DARK CRUCIBLE

THE ARONDIGHT CODEX - BOOK FIVE

NICOLE R. TAYLOR

Dark Crucible **(The Arondight Codex - Book Five)** by **Nicole R. Taylor**

Copyright © 2019 by Nicole R. Taylor

All rights reserved.

No part of this book may be reproduced in any form or by any electronic or mechanical means, including information storage and retrieval systems, without written permission from the author, except for the use of brief quotations in a book review.

www.nicolertaylorwrites.com

Cover Design: Covers by Juan

Edited by: Silvia Curry

PROLOGUE

"She hasn't spoken a word since we picked her up."

I clicked two Lego blocks together—blue and yellow—vaguely aware that I wasn't where I was supposed to be. It wasn't scary. We always went to new places when the scary people came too close.

'It was a road trip,' Mummy said. 'People love to travel.'

Daddy put me in the back of the car and buckled me into the seat, then ruffled my hair. Mummy always gave me a stuffed rabbit to hold, but I didn't need it to feel brave.

I clicked the last piece of Lego onto the top of my castle. It had a tower and a big wall. The colours were all wrong, but they didn't have the right kind of blocks. I didn't ask because I knew that's all they had.

"Will you look at that," a man was saying. He had on a doctor coat—a white one like in the cartoons I'd seen on the telly—and he was old with grey hair and wrinkles. "She's built a whole goddamned castle."

"Do you think she's autistic?" the lady asked. "She seems clever for her age and it would explain her silence."

"She witnessed a horrific crime," the doctor replied. "It could just be the trauma."

"It's such a shame." She clucked her tongue. "If we can't find her family, she'll go into the system."

"It's out of our hands, Barbara. I don't like it, either, but it's the law."

"A child with her intelligence should be nurtured, not thrown into foster care. She'll slip through the cracks, Mark."

The man sighed. "She's not the first and she won't be the last. The system is flawed, but it's all we have." The box clipped to his belt beeped. "Shite. I've got to go to A&E. There's an ambulance coming. Will you be okay until social services arrive?"

The woman nodded. "Yeah. They shouldn't be too far away."

I didn't look at the man as he rushed from the room. I'd already begun taking apart my castle. Not like the demons did, though—I was more careful.

"Honey," the woman said, sitting beside me on the floor.

I didn't really want to talk to her. I wasn't going to be here very long anyway.

"Your mummy and daddy have passed away," she told me. "They've gone to Heaven. Do you know what that means?"

I blinked, wondering why she was asking me about a place that didn't exist. Heaven wasn't like she thought it was—it lived next door like the demons did.

"Do you understand, honey?" the woman prodded.

I nodded. I knew what dead meant.

"Can you tell me your name?" She pointed to herself. "I'm Barbara. I'm a nurse."

"Scarlett," I replied politely. Mummy always said to use my manners, but sometimes it was hard.

"Scarlett. That's a pretty name." She picked up a strand of my hair. "Who coloured your hair?"

She didn't like it, but it didn't matter. That's just the colour my hair was, like some people had blonde or brown or even orange hair. My hair was purple and dark brown. Daddy said it was like grape-chocolate, and Mummy told him not to be silly. There was no such thing as grape-chocolate.

The woman had already expected me not to answer. "Come on. Let's get you a warm shower, huh? We can wash that colour out of your hair."

I'd let her try, though I knew it wouldn't come out. Mummy said it was important to take pride in your appearance. Daddy said it was just a good idea not to smell bad.

By the time the other people came to take me to a new house, I smelled like rose petals and my grape-chocolate hair was braided in pigtails.

Mummy and Daddy were gone. I didn't know where I was going, but I knew I had to wait. I was supposed to do something important.

But I couldn't remember what.

It was the fourth foster family that was the worst.

The guy was a brute who was fluent in the language of violence, and the woman was a pushover who sucked down a packet of cigarettes every single day rather than acknowledge that her husband was a pathetic excuse for a human. She probably thought she couldn't do any better, so she stayed with him rather than acknowledge her fear of being alone— even though she'd be better off.

They didn't care where I went or what I did, only what they could get out of me…which was the extra money in their monthly welfare cheques. It went a long way in developing my sense of worth in the world, which was a malnourished commodity.

Any money I earned from the odd job I managed to hold down at the local takeaway shop always disappeared no matter how hard I tried to hide it. I got fired when I was caught pilfering a chicken drumstick, but I was so hungry. I was lucky to get one meal a day and I never had lunch at school. My clothes and shoes had holes in them, and my school uniform swam on my emaciated body. I hated it when it rained because my socks would soak through.

I was always getting into trouble because of my hair, but the colour never held, no matter how many times I tried to dye over it. Even the darkest black couldn't blot out the purple, so I stopped caring and soon enough, the world stopped caring about me.

School was a pointless exercise, but I went because

I had nowhere else to go.

I stared down at my English exam and rubbed my eyes. The classroom was completely silent, apart from the scratching of pens on paper and the odd cough.

I'd gotten it in my head last night that I should actually try, so I'd done the unthinkable—*I studied*. I'd even lifted a fiver from the fat arsehole who was supposed to look after me but he'd stolen it right back, so I hadn't been able to buy any breakfast.

I knew all the answers; I just couldn't focus. I was hungry, tired, and didn't have the energy to fight anymore. I couldn't believe I'd actually come here wanting to try. What a joke. It was never going to happen.

My stomach rumbled loudly and I glanced around the room. Several kids looked up from their exams and glanced at me, and one or two of them sniggered.

"What?" I demanded, my voice loud in the silence.

The teacher looked up and scowled. "Shut it, Scarlett."

"Yeah, shut it, Scarlett," Sally Mathewson hissed. She smirked and I wanted nothing more than to punch that evil bitch in the face.

Bullies came in every shape and size, but none were fatter and more full of themselves than the most popular girl in the entire school. Her manipulations knew no bounds, and I wasn't her only target, but I was her favourite. I always bit.

"Shut your face, Mathewson," I snarled, throwing my exam paper at her face, "or I'll shut it for you."

And that's how I found myself in the headmaster's office. *Again*.

Mr. Heatherington was looking at me with disapproval. It was a look I'd come to know extremely well, and he wasn't the first authority figure to give it to me.

"You have the ability to go far, Scarlett, but you continue to sabotage yourself. Why is that?"

I shrugged, wanting to be anywhere but here. We kept doing this pointless dance and it was getting real old, real fast.

"Four schools, two expulsions, more suspensions than actual days attended…" He clucked his tongue and shook his head. This time he looked defeated rather than angry. *Welcome to the club, Heatherington.* "Your aptitude tests are the highest in the entire school. You could go really far—"

"Can I go?"

"No." He regarded me for a long moment. "I know you don't have a stable home, Scarlett, but we can help you. We have programs that—"

"No program ever helped me," I interrupted. "No one ever did anything to help me when it counted and it's too late now."

"It's never too late." Even as he said it, I knew he didn't really mean it. It was just a series of words he'd read in a teacher's handbook some place. *Every child is special. Yeah, right.*

"Don't worry, Mr. Heatherington. It's not your fault I'm screwed up. I just got dealt the short straw."

There was no point. The moment I turned

eighteen, I was out of here. No more screwed up foster homes, no more school, and no more system to let me down. I'd be an adult who was legally able to make decisions for herself.

The thought of not having to go back to that stinking house and have all my money stolen sounded like heaven. I could move to London and find work in a pub—those kinds of jobs were always hiring. They had a killer punk scene down there, too. I'd finally be able to find a place I could belong.

The headmaster looked at me and sighed. He'd given up before he'd even really tried, but then again, I wasn't receptive enough to let him. I didn't fit in anywhere I went. I was always the outsider, too weird and too quiet. I didn't fit the mould labelled 'normal,' so no one ever knew where to put me. I didn't even understand what went on in my head half the time, so how could anyone else?

The only place I seemed to belong was in the too hard basket.

"You can go," he said after a moment. "But I don't want to see you back here, do you hear?"

I shoved to my feet and pushed out of the office without a word.

Students were milling around the lockers, gathering their books for the next period. A few people looked up at me, then turned away just as quickly.

"There's the head case now," Sally Mathewson said loudly. "Seriously, someone should lock that bitch up in a padded room."

Her posse laughed, sniggering behind their hands and flashing disgusted looks in my direction.

Something snapped inside—a flash of electricity zapped up and down both arms—and I lost it. I turned and strode towards her with a singular purpose. I raised my fist and slammed it into her perfect nose, sending her hurtling back into the lockers with a bang.

"Say that again!" I shouted. "Say it again and the next punch will break your nose!"

"No one will ever love a freak like you," she hissed, wiping her face. "*Never.*"

She was right, of course. No one could ever love a broken freak like me. I was too far gone to come back. I was a wild creature who was destined to wade in the cesspool of life.

"Do yourself a favour and put yourself out of your misery," she snarled, kicking me in the proverbial guts. "No one will miss you."

I raised my fist again, trembling as I struggled against the anger which coiled inside me.

"Ravenwood!" the headmaster bellowed. "My office! *Now!*"

Like hell. Everyone had a breaking point, and I'd just reached mine. I lowered my fist, turned my back on them, and walked down the hall, freedom only a corridor away.

"Ravenwood! Don't you walk away from me!"

I pushed open the door and breathed in the fresh air.

And I never went back.

1
———

London stretched before me, the orange and white artificial lights obscuring the stars overhead.

My feet dangled over the edge of the roof of the Sanctum and my breath vaporised in plumes. It was November, six months after I'd disappeared through the standing stones and reappeared in the past. Summer and autumn were gone, and winter was inbound, and this year it would be with a vengeance.

I hugged my mass-produced copy of the Codex against my chest and sighed. When I'd told Jackson my time with the knights of Camelot felt like a million years ago, it wasn't a pun. I'd been back a week and there'd been nothing but chaos in my wake.

People watched me with skepticism everywhere I went, none of them believing that I'd travelled through time, let alone that I could be Arondight. I was that outcast kid again, lost and struggling with her lot in life, a hairsbreadth from blowing up and walking away.

Everyone thought I was captured and Wilder… Oh, God. Wilder had gone looking for me and hadn't come back. The last time I'd spoken to him I'd been such a raging bitch, and now he was out there somewhere complete with an MIA tag on his official record and he didn't know… He needed to know who he was.

"You okay?"

I glanced up at the sound of Jackson's voice. He was bundled up in his new favourite outfit—Natural tactical gear with a thick wooden coat. It suited him and his new beefed-up physique, though it wasn't so new anymore.

He sat beside me and glanced at the book. "What are you thinking about?"

"About the day I ran away from my last foster home," I told him. "I punched the school bully in the face and walked out…and kept walking."

"That's quite a specific memory. I thought you would've been thinking about something else."

"Like?"

"The marathon grilling you just endured from the United Nations of Naturals."

"Don't remind me," I groaned. "The last thing I wanted to do was try to convince them of all the things I did or did not change while I was in the past, let alone all the other stuff."

A whole week of standing in front of the council

on teleconference with five other Sanctums—London, New York, Berlin, Sydney, Madrid, and Los Angeles —hadn't eased my anxiety one bit.

One, I hadn't even known there were Sanctums in all those places. And two, they'd all regarded my story with skepticism. Because I hadn't brought back a sword, they were having a hard time wrapping their heads around the idea of Arondight being a living, breathing Natural.

It also didn't help that I'd turned their identity as supernatural demon hunters on its head. There was a thousand years of lost history before the cataclysm, but I wasn't sure that was the part they were having trouble understanding.

Honestly, it could be any number of things. The Druids and their world beyond the Darklands. Avalon being sealed forever. The Lady of the Lake's origin story. My time-traveling Druid prism. The evolution of demonkind from hulking seven-foot-tall monsters to rotting corpses.

But I think it had more to do with the real reason the rift opened underneath Camelot. Arthur and Lancelot had come to blows over the love of Guinevere and had crossed swords—Excalibur and Arondight—and the shockwave tore through space and time. An infinite number of parallel universes existed beside our own—some only slightly different, while others contained hellish landscapes full of demons wanting nothing more than to consume and destroy.

The war between the Light and the Dark, all the death and destruction, had been their greatest heroes' fault—Arthur and Lancelot. I may as well have walked into their posh conference room and left a giant turd on the floor. Galahad had taken it much better, and Lancelot was his father.

"I know you left some things out of your testimony," Jackson said before I could tumble down the rabbit hole of what I'd left behind.

I snorted. "They don't believe a word of what I said. I stopped while the going was only slightly horrifying."

Jackson laughed and kicked his boot against mine. "Since when has that stopped you?"

Never, but the council's grilling had left me with more uncertainties than not. I supposed I couldn't blame them after everything that'd gone down with Wainthrope and Brax, but I wasn't a show pony who could perform on cue. I didn't know what it meant to be Arondight, let alone wield that kind of power.

"I wish Wilder was here," I murmured. "And Galahad. I reached for him, but he didn't come through the portal."

"I'm sure he's okay, Scarlett."

"Is he? How can anyone know? I left him on that hill surrounded by a horde of original demons commanded by Markzoth."

"I don't know the guy, only what you've told me, but he sounds like he knew what he was getting himself into. Arondight was his destiny and he fulfilled it by getting you home."

I hugged the Codex tighter and wondered about the real Codex. If something had happened to Galahad, then it would change, right? So far, Greer hadn't said a word, but I'd hardly seen her since I stumbled home. A small part of me wondered if she blamed me for Wilder's disappearance. Okay, it was a large part, but I was the reason he'd left. Did that mean he cared for me even after he'd requested not to be my partner?

"How *do* you repair space and time?" Jackson wondered out loud.

"Love," I told him. "Arondight and Excalibur were crossed over love and it was jealousy that tore Camelot apart. Our love for one another has to be pure in order to save everyone."

"*Oh...*"

"Yeah," I drawled. "Have you met me and Wilder? We're a big ball of cuteness."

"That's only because he doesn't understand yet. Remember that time I caught you two kissing in the hall?"

I snorted, not wanting to go there. "What if I can't get it together? Wilder's out there someplace, and we have to use love to repair the rift. *Love.* I don't think I'm capable of love."

"I don't believe that," Jackson said as he shook his head. "You had a shitty childhood, that wasn't entirely your fault, but look at you now. You turned out just fine, Scarlett."

I wasn't sure what to think. Were my behavioural problems because of Arondight, or was it because of my humanity? The only thing I did know was that I didn't understand what I'd become and neither did anyone else. It wasn't like the Lady of the Lake had given me a handbook. She'd taken my hands, awoken my power, and sent me on my merry way. I'd Google it, but somehow the chances of getting a hit on 'mystical power from the stars and how to use it' were absolute zero.

"What did the Lady of the Lake say?" Jackson prodded. "Do you feel any different?"

"She said she was from the stars," I told him.

He cocked his head to the side. "Like an alien?"

"No. It was more spiritual than that. She seemed very…ancient. The wise kind of old, you know?"

"Kind of. Like an Elder Scroll."

"And Elder Scroll? What's that?"

"It's a scroll that contains knowledge of all past and future events but can't be read without a severe price. People go mad, blind, and even die."

"That's so not a thing."

"Yeah, it's not. It's from a game, but—"

"It's so not the same," I huffed.

Jackson laughed. "I've missed arguing with you."

"We don't argue."

"No, we wisecrack at one another."

I grimaced and shook my head, too worn down to laugh. Before me, the city shimmered as I let my power trickle into my awareness. I still wasn't sure how I did it, but it was like Gilhana said. I could sense the earth, though in this time it was a blaze of colour that almost blinded me. I blinked and held my breath, and the light began to fade.

"It's hard to know what to do," Jackson said, looking out over the city that had just appeared so colourful to my eyes. "There's still so much going on out there."

"What I do know is that I need to find Wilder. He needs to know the truth." And without him, all was lost.

"And we have to shut down Human Convergence once and for all."

In all the time I'd been away, the alpha site still hadn't been found. The experiments had continued, and infected humans had been turning up left, right, and centre. It was as if the demons knew Arondight had been found and were building their army while I was made to stand in front of a webcam and explain myself.

"I think I can help with that," I said. "If they ever let me out of here."

"How?"

"I can sense things. When I let it in, the city lights up. I'm pretty sure I can use it to pick out the demons from the humans."

"Oh… well, that sounds useful." Jackson didn't understand it either, but at least he wasn't afraid of it like the council was. "Do you see anything funky when you look at me?"

I shrugged. "I don't know. I close it out."

"Is that a good idea? Maybe you should practice?"

"How's Madeleine?" I asked, changing the subject. "I haven't had a chance to see her."

Jackson grimaced at my blatant avoidance. "Good. She understands you're busy. You've got a lot on your mind."

"I worry about her." Knowing what Jackson had gone through, and Wilder growing up, it must be hard for her. She was away from the Academy, her friends, her family, and now the world was imploding around her.

"She's like ninety percent demonic, but her heart and soul are still Natural."

I nodded. "I should have been there for her."

"You can't be all things to all people, Scarlett."

The door opened behind us, saving me from another turn around the downward spiral, and Jackson turned.

"Oh, there you are," a female voice declared. "I've been looking all over."

"Esme," he said, pushing to his feet.

I looked over my shoulder at the illusive Esme, the woman Jackson had saved from Human Convergence while I was at the Academy. I hadn't had the chance to meet her amongst all the chaos of the last seven months—six of them being on crusade in the Middle Ages—but now that I saw her, I understood why Jackson was so smitten.

The light on the roof was murky at best, but I could see her as clear as day. It was another benefit of being a half-mystical being from the stars, I supposed.

Esme Winters was a waifish English beauty. She had long almond-coloured hair that fell in waves around her shoulders, her ivory skin was more natural than the result of the terrible weather, as was the dusting of freckles across her cheeks and nose. She was the complete opposite of me—shy, demure, and proper—and more suited for Jackson if you asked my opinion.

I stood, shoving my book underneath my arm, and held out my hand. "I'm—"

"Scarlett Ravenwood," she declared, beaming at me. "I know. I hoped I'd get the chance to meet you." She grabbed my proffered hand and shook. I stared at her, bewildered, and she let me go. "Oh, I'm sorry! I don't know my own strength. It's been months, but I still forget about the you-know-what."

"No, it's just…"

"People look at her weird," Jackson told her.

"Well, us weirdos have to look out for one another." Her smile widened. "I saw Romy downstairs, and she said Greer was looking for you."

"For me?" I asked with a groan.

"What's wrong?" She looked between us, her smile fading.

"Every time Greer asks for me, it means I'm in trouble," I explained.

"How could you be in trouble? You're like the Harry Potter of the Natural world!"

My eyebrows rose and I covered a smile. Shite, they were perfect for each other.

"You'll find out soon enough," Jackson said wryly.

"Scarlett has a knack for sticking it to the establishment."

Boy, did I ever.

Greer was waiting for me in the conservatory.

The dome was dark, the nighttime sky beyond tinted orange by the artificial glow of London, but the room was illuminated with the old-fashioned lights of the Sanctum. It was an old building that'd been built upon over the years like most of the structures in this part of the city. Amongst the modern improvements there were parts that had seen hundreds years of progress pass them by.

The Codex hummed in its glass enclosure, the Light it emitted more potent now that I was awakened as Arondight. It'd always called to me, but now it seemed to scream for my attention.

"Scarlett," Greer said, beckoning me up the stairs, "thank you for coming so late."

It was past ten, though it seemed early for a Natural. Demons loved lurking in darkness, so patrolling had become a nocturnal endeavour.

"Has there been news from the council?" I asked.

"No. They'll be arguing amongst themselves for months. This is far more interesting than that lot of hot air."

I snorted at her frankness. I kind of liked this no-holes-barred version of the protector of the Codex and hoped she replaced the uptight woman I always seemed to butt heads with.

She stepped through the glass encasing the pedestal where the Codex sat. "Come and see."

Greer was inviting me to read the Codex? Usually I had to go behind her back.

Shrugging, I stood beside her and looked down on the book, the vibrations making my brain throb. I managed to shut it out, just like I had the lights in the city and was glad I was working out how to use some of my new abilities, no matter how small.

She'd opened the Codex to a page near the beginning, where some of the first stories had been written by the Naturals of Camelot—the same people I'd met only recently. It was an illuminated image, drawn by hand and inlaid with gold leaf. An image of Camelot torn in two by silver and violet flames was at the top and small, flowery text was below.

"I don't recognise this page," I murmured.

"Exactly. Some...*alterations* have appeared since your return."

I glanced at the book and wondered if Percival had heard about my suggestions from Bedivere. Greer was the protector of the Codex, so I supposed she'd know if something had truly changed.

"Alterations?" I asked with a frown.

"It's just as you said," she murmured. "Our origins, the cataclysm, even the Lady of the Lake..."

I ran my fingers over the pages, no longer afraid of what it might do to me. "They changed it..."

"It seems whatever you said to our ancestors, they took notice."

"You believe me?" I asked her. "The other councils—"

"The other councils don't know you. They're so far removed from what's happening here, they can't. Unfortunately, they have their own problems in their own cities. We live in a global society and most of them haven't even left their home country. England and Camelot are so far away from what they know, even though it is their birthright as it is ours."

I lowered my gaze and studied the new illuminations depicting the truth of the cataclysm. I wondered if it was just us who were reading these new pages, or the Naturals over the centuries had seen them, too.

"Scarlett, whatever once passed between us, I hope we can leave in the past," Greer went on. "There is no protocol that can contain Arondight."

I snorted. "Or Scarlett Ravenwood."

Greer laughed, and I no longer cared that it sounded like angels singing every time she opened her mouth. "No, there isn't."

I closed the Codex and stepped out of the glass enclosure. "Greer, I need to leave the Sanctum."

"I know, that's why I'm ignoring the recommendations of the committee and putting my faith in you. It's clear from the moment you returned that something was awoken inside you. Aldrich and I will not put any restrictions on your movements… within reason, of course. If it's as you say, then we must find Wilder and only you can do that. What was it you said about the Twin Flames?"

"We will always be linked because of who we are," I told her. "Any leads you can give me would be greatly appreciated."

"If you speak to Aldrich, he's collected all the reports and statements for you."

"Greer, I know you and Wilder—"

"It's okay," she interrupted. "Our relationship was never meant to be anything long term. I know that now and so does he." She paused as if to let the notion sink in. "Please don't take his choice to not be your partner personally. He struggles with his emotions and his place here."

"I think we both understand why now."

Greer grimaced. "He cares deeply for you, Scarlett. When you never came back, he was… Well, he was beside himself with worry. That's why he left against orders to search for you himself."

That sounded familiar. Seemed like a reckless thing an unknown power lodged inside him would make him do.

"Was it for me, or for Arondight?"

"*For you.*"

That meant a lot coming from Greer, and I began to feel Wilder's absence more keenly.

The sound of boots on the wrought iron stairs drove us to silence. I was expecting a Natural in tactical gear or Aldrich to appear, but to my surprise, it was Aiden, the librarian slash historian from the Academy…which was where he should be.

"Scarlett!" He crossed the room to meet me in all his nerdy glory.

"Aiden!" I threw my arms around his neck and held on for dear life. I was glad to see him, no matter where he was.

"I'm so glad you're okay."

"It's so good to see you," I murmured. "I'm sorry."

"Sorry?" he asked, pulling back. "What in the world for?"

"For showing up like I did, then vanishing."

"Forget about it," he said. "When they said you'd gone missing, I knew I should've gone with you." We both knew Aiden Thompson wasn't the fighter of the family, but I appreciated the sentiment. "We searched the woods for weeks but couldn't find any trace of you."

"The Druids tricked me into going back in time," I explained, knowing he'd want to pick my brain over it.

"And you were Arondight all this time!" Word spread fast, it seemed.

"Is that the definition of irony, because it sure feels like it," I drawled.

Greer coughed behind us. "Should I leave you to it?"

"Oh, my goodness. Is that…" Aiden stared at the Codex, his eyes wide.

I grasped his shoulders. "Aiden, *breathe*." He took a deep breath and Greer hid a smile at his fanboy reaction. "It's the middle of the night. Is something wrong?"

"I came as soon as I realised what this was," he explained, taking out a folded piece of parchment. It looked old—yellowed with age. "The strangest thing happened with the suit of armour in the library."

"Galahad's armour?" I asked, my heart leaping into my throat.

"Yeah, the gauntlet fell off. Made a huge bang that scared me half to death. When I picked it up, I found this inside." He handed me the paper. "I didn't know what it was," he rambled on. "I read it and… Well, it seems to be for you."

I unfolded it, my hands shaking.

Dear Scarlett,

I hope my words find you in your mysterious future. It's the only way I could think to reach you. I want you to know that I made it back to Castle Brent safely. I couldn't come with you, but the name you gave me secured my escape.

We will endure and secure the lineage so you are able to fulfil your destiny. I believe in you, the insane woman with purple hair from the future.

My heart is always and forever yours,
Galahad.

I held the paper to my chest and allowed the tears to fall from my eyes. *Galahad…*

"He made it," I whispered, grasping Greer's shoulders and shaking her. "Galahad made it!"

She looked bewildered for a moment and laughed when I did the same to Aiden.

Galahad survived and my heart felt at ease. Now I just had to find Wilder and awaken Excalibur.

"Soooo…" Aiden said, flashing some serious side eye at the Codex. "Since I'm here anyway—"

"Would you like to look upon the book?" Greer asked.

His eyes lit up like a pair of Christmas trees. "*Would I?*"

2

———

I found Aldrich in the gym.

Peering into a private room, I spied him going through drills with a staff. He pivoted, bringing around his weapon of choice in a slow, smooth arc. The patterns were like a complex meditation and seeing him go through the motions had me missing my training sessions with Wilder.

He had on a black tank top and tactical pants, and his feet were bare. His arm muscles had muscles, and I raised my eyebrow. For an old dude, Aldrich had game, but he was my uncle so…*awkward.*

I rapped on the door and he turned, relaxing when he saw me.

"Scarlett."

"You're training late."

"Ah," he said with a shrug. "It's a good stress reliever."

"Greer said you had some paperwork for me."

He sniffed and grabbed his towel. Dabbing at his

sweaty forehead, he nodded towards the pile on the bench. It seemed as if he knew I wouldn't be able to help myself and had brought it along to his late-night training session.

I opened my mouth to ask him about his sister, but something made me hesitate. Andromeda was my mother, but she'd also been brutally hunted and ultimately murdered by Markzoth. I was his only surviving family, but the knowledge came with a heavy price.

"That's everything we have," he added. "There were numerous patrols and search parties, and I collated all their reports. I'm not sure how helpful it will be, but with your new abilities, perhaps you can see whatever it is that we missed."

"I hope so. I really don't understand what's happened to me." I sat on the bench and picked up the first manila folder. "Everything's different, but it's… Cloudy somehow."

Aldrich sat beside me, the stack of reports between us. "We're in uncharted territory. The only way through is to forge on. *Following the light of the sun, we left the Old World.*"

"Who said that?"

"Christopher Columbus."

I shook my head. I'd been expecting him to quote some old Natural warrior, but here he was drawing inspiration from humanity.

"I wonder what they felt, the people who did things no one else had the courage to do. The explorers and inventors of the world," he mused.

Aldrich was trying to inspire me like the wise uncle I always wish I'd had growing up. Courage was obviously underrated.

"There's something I've been meaning to talk to you about…" I trailed off, knowing there was no easy way to tell him what happened to his sister.

"Is everything all right?" He seemed to sense the shift in my mood. "I know that's a loaded question given the circumstances, but you can come to me with anything."

I couldn't hold it in any longer. "Andromeda was my birth mother," I blurted.

Aldrich tensed, his gaze meeting mine. "Are you certain?"

"Yes. I was too young to remember her, but the closer I came to awakening as Arondight, the more I saw her in my dreams."

"Your dreams?"

I nodded.

"That means…" His eyes were getting misty, which was odd to see from such a stoic man.

"You're my uncle."

He stared at the mat for so long, I was starting to wonder if he regretted how I'd come into the world. After all, it was me who'd led to Andromeda's death.

"I'm sorry…" I said. "If I wasn't who I was—"

"No," he interrupted, taking my hand in his. "What happened to her, her choices… It wasn't your fault, Scarlett. It makes so much sense now. She left to protect you and our future. It had to be this way."

I scoffed, "It doesn't make it feel any better."

"No one said saving the world would be easy." Or righting past wrongs. "I see so much of her in you," he told me. "She was a talented fighter, headstrong, rebellious, dedicated…"

"Really?" I turned towards him, grabbing onto any shred of information he could give me.

"When her arondight blade chose you, I didn't dare to hope."

Neither did I, because I'd been let down again and again. But the past was the past and nothing we could do could change it.

"Maybe you knew my father?" I asked.

"Your father?"

"All I know is his name…Chris."

I described him to Aldrich, painting a picture of the man I'd seen in my dreams so many times. Tall, broad shoulders, dusky blond hair with a no-nonsense approach, how he fought and kept us safe…and how he'd loved my mother, Mea.

"Chris Acton," he said with a frown. "That's the only Chris I know that Mea would have ran with."

"You're frowning," I declared. "Why are you frowning?"

"Well, he wasn't exactly a Natural who liked to do things by the book. I remember he had it thrown at him more often than not. His lack of respect reminds me of… Well, it reminds me of Wilder."

"*Great.*" I snorted and shook my head. Apparently, my penchant for troubled men was genetic.

"I'll see if I can find a photograph of him. If he

matches the man in your dreams, then we can go from there.”

“Thanks, Aldrich.” I gathered up the reports on Wilder and rose to my feet.

“Don’t worry about what the other councils say,” he said, the declaration coming out of nowhere. “Greer and I have your back. You might go about things—”

“The wrong way?”

“Yes, well…” He coughed. “You haven’t led us astray. What happens next is entirely up to you.” He stood and grasped my shoulders with his big hands. “Scarlett, you are Arondight. I don’t need a council to tell me that, I can see it just by looking at you. My sister gave her life to protect you and I would do the same *regardless*. You have my full support.”

“You don’t know how much that means to me,” I whispered, my throat tightening.

Aldrich drew me into his arms and held me close, the embrace uncharacteristically intimate for a warrior like him.

“The fate of our world lies on your shoulders, Scarlett, but you aren’t alone. You’re my niece, but you’re also the closest thing I’ve ever had to having a daughter of my own.”

I didn’t want to let him go. He symbolised everything I’d ever wanted, but somehow, I’d found an entire family along the way. It didn’t matter that they weren’t blood related—the London Naturals were still my brothers and sisters.

I relished the moment, but I knew it was simply

the calm before the storm.

———

I couldn't sleep.

Holing up in the library, I'd spread out across an entire alcove. Papers were littered all over the floor and couch, even on my lap.

There were reports on the search the Naturals had undertaken across the city. They'd been everywhere. Brixton—which had been a site of unrest before I'd travelled back in time—Shoreditch, Hammersmith, Finsbury Park, Turnpike Lane, Clerkenwell, and even as far as Croydon in the south and Enfield in the north. The entire city and surrounding area had been scoured, but even I knew if someone wanted to hide something in London, then there was no end of secret hidey holes to scurry into.

Something or someone had captured him, or…

I knew what everyone was thinking but there was no way in hell Wilder was dead. It'd been six months, but if anyone could survive that long with demons on his tail, it was him. The only other person I knew with those kinds of skills was Galahad.

"Hey."

I looked up, bleary eyed, to find Hunter lingering at the edge of the alcove. He looked different from the last time I'd seen him—when he'd almost gotten possessed by an Infernal on his first patrol with me. That was six months ago, but it didn't feel that way to me.

Hunter had been a clean-cut, hipster of a Natural, but I could see his cockiness had entirely worn off. His dusty blond hair was longer and fell into his eyes, his jaw was covered with an impressive five o'clock shadow, and he had a serious air about him…almost like he'd seen enough of the bad side of our world to have it grate against his soul like sandpaper.

His gaze raked over the mess I'd made, but he didn't mention it.

"You're a hard woman to track down, even in this time period," he said, his American accent almost alien to my ears. I was so used to hanging out with Brits that he felt a few decibels too loud.

"I know Greer had said 'within reason', but I didn't know that it included a partner."

Hunter grimaced. "I have no idea what you're talking about."

"Well, then you've got balls."

"Our last encounter was memorable in that it totally humiliated me," he said, scratching his head.

"You look rough," I told him, not wanting to dwell on it.

"Thanks," he drawled. "You look even more purple than ever."

I smirked. How could I still be mad at the guy? He'd been here long enough to know just how dire things were getting. Demon possessions, attacks, and sightings were at an all-time high and only seemed to be increasing. They knew Arondight had been awakened, but how much they understood was another thing entirely.

I raised my eyebrows. "Is there something you wanted to ask me?"

"You're going to look for Wilder, and I want to go with you."

That made me pause. "Why?"

He shrugged. "Why not?"

I sighed. I didn't know if I was tired, overwhelmed, or just whelmed.

Hunter was determined, though. "Look, I know you probably don't need me now that you're all super-powered, but aren't we stronger together?"

Holding a report from Romy in my hands, I thought about Galahad, Bedivere, and the knights of Camelot. Things had been so simple back then, but the real work hadn't even begun, even though the turmoil and danger had been more than real.

Hunter was right. We were stronger together.

"There's nothing in these reports." I began to pick them up and shove the papers back into their folders. "Whatever search was done, it was a waste of time."

Hunter nodded. "There was no trace of him. It was as if he'd vanished off the face of the Earth…just like you did." He coughed and helped me scoop up the chaos on the floor. "Do you think he went back in time like you did?"

I shook my head. "It doesn't feel like it. The Lady of the Lake said I had to go back and find him. The stones brought me to the present, so he has to be here."

"The Lady of the Lake?"

I kept forgetting just how long ago she'd left this

world. To the Naturals, she was something akin to a goddess, an almost mythical being that had guided us against our fight with the Dark. We knew the truth now, but it seemed I'd been the last person to lay eyes on her. Avalon was sealed, the Druids had disappeared for their paradise, and the Naturals were left to clean up their mess.

Wilder and I were the only two people left that bore any resemblance to the Lady's long-lost people. The Naturals wielded barely a drop of her power.

"I've tracked his supposed movements," I went on. Explaining the Lady would take all day—literally, because it was daylight outside. I'd been here all night, but I didn't feel tired anymore. "He went to the Academy and assisted with the search for me in the Cotswolds, then came back to the city and resumed it here. His last report mentioned nothing of interest, though he scoured some locations he believed housed the demon laboratory known as the alpha site." The home of the Human Convergence Project which Jackson and Ramona were so desperate to find.

"So we start from scratch," Hunter said.

I shook my head. "Going over old ground won't help anyone."

"Then what do you suggest?"

I looked up at him and knew there was only one thing I could do—call out for my Twin Flame.

Hunter's lips curved. He was on the same wavelength and I wondered if I was starting to like the guy. He looked at me like I used to look at Wilder —which was in awe of the things he could do. I supposed it was time to figure out just how bad arse Arondight could be.

"Get some rest," I told him. "We leave as soon as the sun goes down."

<hr>

The city was awash with colour. My awareness level was vibrating on a higher plane of existence. Well, it was either that or I was hurtling headfirst into a k-hole.

Hunter and I walked through the streets of Westminster, weaving through the masses of foot traffic. Big Ben was clad in scaffolding, the iconic clock well and truly in the midst of restoration, and red double-decker busses zoomed back and forth over the bridge. Across the Thames, the London Eye rotated slowly, and the lights of the aquarium pulsed blue.

The chilly weather hadn't kept the tourists at bay, nor the panhandlers and gypsies who liked to linger at either end of the bridge.

As if all that colour wasn't enough, I could see a whole other layer like I was peering through a sheet of holographic cellophane. The woman we just passed had a green glow radiating around her head, the man behind her was blue, and the woman trying to sell little flowers with aluminum foil wrapped around the stems was an earthy mix of brown and yellow.

I wondered if the strange glow was people's auras.

I'd never really thought about it before, dismissing that kind of new-age stuff as mumbo jumbo. However, after the things I'd seen in the past year, I wasn't so sure anymore.

Amongst the rainbow of the human race, I found no silver. I also found nothing sinister, which didn't bode well. Could the demons sense who I was and had scurried back into their holes? I didn't know, but there was no trace suggesting Wilder had ever been here.

Not that I knew what I was looking for.

Turning, a burst of bright yellow erupted in my vision as I bumped into a man walking the other way. He glared at me, but I could hardly see his face. I stepped aside, but a splash of pink and violet splattered across my vision, blinding me.

I darted into a dark alley, pressed my forehead against the cool limestone, and squeezed my eyes shut.

"Scarlett?" Hunter lingered beside me, and I could sense he was scanning the surrounding space as much as he was watching me.

How could I know that? My bloody my eyes were closed. Was that a thing I could do now? I'd been dumped headfirst into the deep end with zero training and I was struggling to stay afloat. Swords slashed and hacked, but I was a living person.

I thought this was supposed to be easy. I contained the power to save the world, yet I still struggled.

"I can see them all," I murmured.

"Who?"

"Everyone. Their colours."

"Colours?" He was silent for a moment, then proclaimed, "Auras."

"There's just too many. I can't see through them…"

"C'mon." He held out his hand.

I still had my eyes closed, but I knew the gesture was there and it freaked me out even more. I hesitated for a long moment before I slipped my palm against his.

He took me farther down the river where it was darker. The foot traffic was less here, and I was finally able to take a deep breath.

"I forgot how many people lived here," I murmured, watching the lights ripple across the water.

"The past was that calming, huh?"

"I don't know what's worse—social media or the Black Plague."

Hunter snorted and shook his head. "Living life through a screen, huh?"

"It's easy for us to say. We don't have time for selfies."

He leaned against the railing and glanced at me. "Feel better?"

"Don't tell anyone about this or I'll string you up by the balls."

"You got it." He laughed and shook his head. "So, the Lady of the Lake just flipped your switch on and sent you out into the world, huh?"

"Something like that." I snorted. "It's not like

there's an instruction manual. I guess I'm just supposed to know."

"Well, no one knows who they really are, at least not to begin with. It takes a lot of trial and error."

"You say that like you never wanted to be a Natural."

"We don't get to choose what we are. I'll always be a Natural, but a warrior?" He shrugged. "It wasn't my first choice."

"Then what was?"

"Sheesh." He bristled and looked me over, but I sensed he was just trying to lighten my load. "Are you Brits always so forthright?"

"This life has taught me how to be direct. I guess I'm more aware of my mortality now that I know demons from a parallel universe are running around possessing everyone."

"I guess I never really knew what I wanted to be," Hunter stated. "I trained because that's what we did."

"And now?"

He grinned and shoved a hand through his hair. "I'm standing here with Arondight, so what do you think?"

"Unwarranted."

"I believe in you, and so does everyone at the London Sanctum. You want to know what I think?"

"Not really, but I suspect you're going to tell me anyway."

"Stop trying to be everything all at once."

I breathed deeply and turned my back on the river.

Closing my eyes, I focused on the spark of Light inside me. It was there just as it always had been, waiting for me to reach out and tap into it—purple, glowing, tempting.

Had anything really changed? Did knowing I was Arondight stop me from being the same Scarlett that had bailed Hunter out that night in Brixton? The things I'd done while tapping into the shard was just an extension of my true self. The only thing that was different now was that I was aware.

Aware.

I peeled away from the physical and soared. The city was a rainbow swirl below me, and the stars shone above. Looking down over humanity, I searched for Wilder, hoping I could spot the telltale silver spark that would tell me he still lived, but I saw something else I wasn't expecting.

A blind spot of blood. Like a shadow figure that was only present out the corner of your eye; the moment I looked at it, it disappeared. A sickness was spreading across the city and it was emanating from a spot of darkness that should be full of light. The more my consciousness circled it, the more nauseous I felt.

It was the alpha site, it had to be. If they thought they could hide from Arondight, they were sorely mistaken.

I opened my eyes and looked at Hunter with renewed energy.

"What?" he asked, his brows knitting together.

"Demons," I replied. "And I know where they are."

3

———

I burst into the conservatory, Aldrich and Greer turning to face the whirlwind coming towards them.

"I know where the alpha site is," I declared.

They stared at me, both of them sporting impressive frowns.

"I'm sorry," Hunter said, trailing behind me. "I tried to stop her, but you try to tell Arondight no."

"By now, I've given up attempting to explain the chain of command to Scarlett," Greer said, her gaze turning towards me.

"The alpha site?" Aldrich asked. Whatever he and Greer had been discussing seemed to be forgotten.

"It's a cesspool of Darkness downwind from the toilet bowl otherwise known as the alpha site," I told them. "It has to be."

"You've got a real way with words," Greer observed.

Aldrich sighed, clearly used to me by now. "Dare I ask how you found it?"

"I can sense things now," I explained. "See things others can't."

The conservatory fell silent. I knew I was asking them to take too much on faith, but how could I explain something no one else could see?

"It's the only lead we have," Aldrich said to Greer. "We could at least scout the location and if it proves to be fruitful…"

Greer stared at him for a long moment, silently deliberating, then said, "Agreed. If there's an opportunity to disable Human Convergence, we should take it. We've been at a stalemate with the Dark for far too long."

"Hunter," Aldrich gestured to him, "assemble the team. Keep it small. Scarlett and I will meet you in the armoury shortly."

Hunter nodded and strode from the conservatory, leaving me alone with Aldrich and Greer. The Codex hummed happily in its glass enclosure and I glanced at it.

"Scarlett, are you sure what you saw was linked to Human Convergence?" Aldrich asked.

"I don't know what else it could be," I replied. "I have nothing else to compare it to, but a whole city block is infected by a black hole of Darkness. If you've got any other ideas, I'd love to hear them."

He shook his head. "Demonic activity has been steadily increasing, but not like this."

"This felt like more than a concentration of

possessions or demonic essences. There was…" I frowned, "well, there was something painful about it."

"Could it be a greater demon's lair?" he mused.

"We won't know until we go," I said.

"It's worth the risk," Greer reiterated. "Whatever you do, be safe."

Aldrich nodded towards the stairs. We left Greer with the Codex and made our way down to the armoury to meet Hunter and the other Naturals he'd gathered. The New Yorker had really stepped up around here if Aldrich trusted him enough to put together strike teams.

As I moved around the racks of weapons, I was surprised to see Jackson and Esme arming themselves with daggers. They couldn't use any of the arondight blades, but cold iron wasn't an exclusive Natural thing.

"What are you doing?"

"You're not the only one who gets to train around here," Jackson said with a smirk.

"He's pretty good," Esme declared.

"I can't help but see that you're armed to the teeth, too."

"These are dangerous times, Scarlett," Jackson said. "What use is having super strength and demon abilities if we can't use them against the sadistic sons of bitches who did this to us in the first place?"

"We've been looking for the alpha site for months," Esme went on. "We need to dismantle their operation, but we also need any information we can get."

"There are still others we need to help out there, too," Jackson said. "It's not going to end just because we blow up their base of operations. The virus is still out there, percolating in a bunch of Infernals."

I shuddered. "Well, when you put it like that…"

"Everyone ready?" Aldrich barked, shoving his arondight blade into the loop of his belt. "We're moving out."

<hr />

I led the strike team across London to the stark and empty financial district.

At this time of night, the streets were empty save for a lone bus or car zooming past on their way to who knows where.

My breath vaporised in the chilly air as I looked up at the echo of Darkness above. It was even more potent at close range than when I'd seen it from above. Black gunk oozed from cracks in the stonework and underneath the windowsills, but of course, it wasn't really there. It was a psychic manifestation of what lingered here, or at least that's what I figured it was.

"Here?" Hunter asked.

I nodded. "Third floor. I can sense it like a putrid fart."

"Charming," Thompson drawled.

"Scarlett and I will take point," Aldrich commanded. "Hunter and Thompson take the rear. Esme and Jackson will keep to the centre. We move quickly and quietly. Assess the area as needed. If it's clear, we gather intelligence. If not, we neutralise."

The Naturals drew their arondight blades, keeping them sheathed in their hilts. I took my place next to Aldrich as he forced the lock on the entrance with his Light.

We moved into the foyer, our boots treading softly on the tiled floor as we moved to the stairs on the left-hand side of a reception area. Silver lettering was fixed to the wall behind the desk, naming the company as *Divergence Laboratories*. The logo appeared to be something similar to a demonic rune I'd seen amongst the books I'd studied at the Academy, and I wondered how this place had gone under the radar for so long. It was just sitting here, operating like a normal business with a brazen calling card.

It'd been hidden, just like the Necropolis, but we hadn't done anything to reveal it. Something smelt fishy…

We moved up the stairs to the third floor, bypassing a retina and thumb print scanner, which Aldrich jammed both with Light. Behind the security measures was the main laboratory, and as we crossed the threshold, I felt the pungent presence of Human Convergence.

The entire place looked as if it'd been full to the brim with technicians and scientists only minutes ago. Slides were still in the microscopes, papers were strewn across countertops, laptops were open and in sleep mode, though someone had shut off the lights.

I frowned and stepped into the room, the others

following me. Darkness coated every inch of this place like thick slime. If I focused, I could see the sticky fingerprints the demons had left behind as if I was holding up a blacklight over a crime scene.

I wondered if this was how the Lady of the Lake saw the world. It would explain why she'd isolated herself in Avalon, and I couldn't blame her. All these new details were overwhelming, even for me.

"This is it," I said, looking over the equipment.

"Scarlett's right," Esme said, peering into a microscope.

"They left in a hurry," Aldrich noted, moving deeper into the lab. "And had enough time to turn out the lights."

"There's a fifty-fifty chance this is an ambush," I declared.

Aldrich nodded his agreement. "Stay sharp, everyone." He clicked his fingers and Hunter and Thompson began to do a sweep. "Jackson, Esme, collect what information you can. You've got five minutes, then we're destroying Human Convergence once and for all."

"Aye, aye, Captain," Jackson said with a salute, then he pulled equipment from his backpack.

I snorted and tightened my grip on my arondight hilt, following Thompson and Hunter. As I walked around the main laboratory, I found a window at the back of the facility. Standing next to it, I squinted into the darkness. Some kind of room lay beyond and the longer I looked at it, the more detail began to ease out of the gloom.

A stainless-steel table was bolted to the floor with numerous restraints hanging from either side. I hissed, realising I'd just found the place where the demons had conducted their experiments on humans. Turning my back, I was glad we were about to blow this place to smithereens.

Aldrich was assisting Jackson and Esme with transferring data with his Light. Remembering how Wilder had stored reams of the stuff on the troll doll he'd given me, I smiled. Who needed bulky hard drives when you had Light?

"Do you feel that?" Jackson dropped what he was doing and looked around the laboratory.

"Feel what?" Aldrich asked as I cast out my senses.

"Demons," I hissed, reaching for my sword.

Infernals swarmed out of every orifice they'd been infecting and swirled around the room in a burst of Darkness which sent the surrounding Naturals into confusion. The demonic essence oozed out of the air-conditioning ducts, appeared from within cupboards, hissed out of the autoclave, and slithered underneath the doors. They forced us into the centre of the laboratory like an angry swarm of electrified bees.

We'd disturbed the nest all right, but I had the strangest feeling they'd been waiting for us.

"They set us up," I declared, my lip curling. "*The arseholes.*"

"I guess we know which fifty percent this is now," Thompson drawled.

The Infernals swirled faster before they broke apart, rushing towards us. Aldrich twisted and shoved

Esme to the side, the demon scraping by her with centimetres to spare. Jackson took out his dagger and swiped at a cloud rocketing towards him, and I sprung into action.

My arondight blade burst into life, violet sparks scattering across the floor as the links locked together. Silver sparks joined the fray as Hunter and Thompson readied themselves.

The Infernals attacked in waves, their comrades not seeming to care when we cut through them like butter. A ball of flame erupted next to my head as Hunter stabbed and another as he swung the other way.

We'd broken apart as more and more Infernals emerged from the ducts, filling the room with Darkness. They were impaling themselves on our blades in an attempt to overwhelm us with their sheer numbers.

"The hell with this," I cursed, filling my blade with a little help from Arondight.

Flame licked down the length of steel, illuminating the laboratory in an eerie glow. The world seemed to slow down, the swirling Infernals became sluggish as I broke away from the others. I raised my sword and swung, cutting through essence after essence, sending the demons into oblivion faster than they had arrived.

Demons swirled, catching me in the eye of a storm of angry shadows, and I flung my arms out. Indigo flame burst from my fingertips and engulfed the swarm. Heat twisted around me but was gone as quickly as it had erupted, taking the Infernals with it.

Sensing a wad of Darkness behind me, I turned just as the essence slammed into Thompson. His head snapped back, and he gagged as the demon took hold.

Cursing, I stepped forwards as he swung his arondight blade. I knew he didn't think that much of me, but bloody hell. I dodged to the side and smashed the hilt of my own sword against the side of his head. He stumbled and I grabbed him around the neck.

I hadn't used Arondight like this before, but I hoped it worked because there was no time to perform an exorcism.

I tightened my grip and pushed a bolt of indigo flame into his body. He jerked as if I'd shocked him, then gagged violently.

I let him go with a curse as black smoke poured out of his mouth, the mass rushing towards the ceiling. With a flick of my wrist, I sliced my Arondight blade through the demon and it exploded into a ball of flame.

Thompson was on his knees, gasping for air. *"Bloody hell."*

"You're welcome."

His eyes widened and he exclaimed, "Behind you!"

Sensing the danger, I twisted and cut through a writhing black mass. It exploded into a ball of flame, the heat radiating against my cheek as I turned away.

"You're welcome," Thompson said, pushing to his feet. "Now we're even."

I snorted and turned to the others, who were back to back in the centre of the laboratory. Aldrich and Hunter had made short work of the other Infernals, and Jackson and Esme were busy packing away their finds to take back to Ramona.

"More will be on their way," I said. "We need to blow this place and get back to the Sanctum."

"That was a piss poor performance on their part," Thompson stated. "Something else is going on here."

"Agreed." Aldrich gestured to Hunter. "Gather outside and wait for us. Scarlett and I will take care of the rest."

The American Natural led the others out of the laboratory to the street below as Aldrich and I were left to contemplate the best path to destruction for a project that had wrought so much suffering to the world. Jackson and Esme had suffered through painful mutations, Madeleine had almost lost everything—she barely had any Light after Human Convergence had taken her—and many other innocent humans had been taken up as servants to the Dark or had died in the process. To put an end to the evil was satisfying beyond belief.

If only Wilder was here…

I shook my head and held out my right hand, aiming for the centre of the room. "What's your poison?" I asked Aldrich. "Slow burn or smoking crater?"

"Smoking crater sounds satisfying, but I'd like to get out of here with my life, if possible."

I smirked and held out my left hand. "I have a feeling I can help you with both those things."

He shrugged and slipped his palm against mine. "Who am I to doubt Arondight or my niece?"

I focused, indigo flame pooling in my free hand and I let it go, sending it into the centre of the laboratory. The explosion tore through the building as I pulled us out of the carnage—a split-second was all it took to bring us outside. We landed beside the others in a gust of violet sparks and they jumped, not knowing where to look.

"Cool," Jackson breathed.

"Yeah? That was the first time I tried that," I declared.

Aldrich coughed loudly and frowned at me. "Next time, remind me to choose the slow burn option."

We watched the flames take hold of the building, our Light containing the blaze so it wouldn't spread. It would burn out with minimal fuss with emergency services none the wiser.

"It was too easy," I said. "It *was* the alpha site we just turned to toast, right?"

"It was," Esme confirmed. "Everything was there —samples, research, testing facilities—"

"There was no reason for it to be deserted like that," Jackson added. "Unless…"

"Unless they were willing to abandon the project," Hunter stated.

"They'd only do that if they had something else up their sleeve," Esme argued. "But they don't, do they?"

My blood ran cold and I looked at Aldrich. "It *was* a trap," I murmured. "But not for us."

Thompson turned. "What do you mean?"

"They know about Arondight," Aldrich said, his gaze meeting mine. "They needed you elsewhere."

"*The Sanctum*," I hissed and took off down the street at a full sprint, my heart in my throat.

"Scarlett! Wait!"

Like hell I was waiting around. Memories flooded my mind of the breech led by Markzoth and the destruction that'd torn through the building. He'd tried to take Greer and the Codex, but Wilder and I had managed to stop him before things went too far.

But Markzoth was dead. It couldn't be the One—he was locked away in his own world—so why now? Even as I asked myself the question, I knew the answer.

I was different. Arondight had been found.

They were making their move.

I wasn't sure how long I'd been running, but the city flashed past, the colours blurring together as my boots struck the footpath. When I came to the Thames, I could feel the others behind me, but ahead was a blight that felt as if it was tearing though my flesh.

I could see the smoke and the ominous glow of flames as we crossed the bridge towards Battersea. Movement ahead made me stop and I gasped as I saw Naturals running towards us, bloodied and covered in grit.

Some were support staff, nurses and doctors under

Ramona's guidance, and other warriors. Greer was amongst them, a man named Lewis was holding her upright. She limped towards us, a look of absolute hopelessness on her face.

"Aldrich!" she cried as she saw us standing on the bridge. "Aldrich!"

"Greer, my God…" He grasped her underneath the arms, taking her weight from Lewis.

"They attacked without warning," she said, grasping her bloodied arm. "Berlin, Rome, New York, Sydney, Los Angeles…"

Hunter tensed beside me. "New York?"

"The warnings started to come through, but… There was an explosion and—" She choked back a sob. "They're gone. *They're all gone.*"

"How does she know?" Hunter asked me, shaking my arm. "My family was in New York…"

"Greer is connected to the Codex, and the Codex is connected to all of us," I said, not understanding how I knew. The amount of Light poured into it over the last eight hundred years had built up until it was so entwined with those who had written it that it was irrevocably connected to those who came after. Arondight sensed it, and I suspected it was part of the reason it had called to me so strongly. "It's more than a book…it's a part of our bloodlines. It knows."

"It knows?" Esme perked up.

"Scarlett's right," Greer said. "As long as the Codex survives, I'm connected to all of us. It's like the cataclysm. We were arrogant, Aldrich. We thought we could flight forever and maintain the balance, but we were wrong."

"Why didn't you tell me?" Aldrich murmured, holding her close. "If you're connected—"

"I'm the protector," she whispered. It wasn't for anyone but her to know. "Whatever's leading them… It's something more powerful than I've ever felt."

"The protocols?" he asked, grasping her shoulders.

She shook her head, her eyes wide with fear. "Aldrich… the Codex…"

I looked up at the Sanctum, my power crackling inside, wanting to be let out.

"The protocols?" Jackson asked. "What protocols?"

"I think she means the self-destruct button," Esme replied.

The Codex was still inside the Sanctum. If the demons got their hands on it, they'd know all our secrets. What else hadn't Greer told us about? If she was connected to Naturals everywhere, could they use it to hunt us to extinction? Could they find me and Wilder? With the Twin Flames in their grasp and no one left to stand in their way, the world was toast.

I closed my fist around my arondight blade and took a step towards the Sanctum.

"Scarlett!" Jackson shouted after me and I turned, the wind stirring my hair.

Snow was beginning to fall, but I wasn't quite sure if it was ice or ash which frosted my shoulders.

"Where are you going?" he asked.

"To get the Codex."

"Scarlett," Greer called out, "you don't understand—"

"No. You don't understand," I told her. "This is what I was born for."

Turning, I walked away from my friends and into the smoking ruin with one thing on my mind.

Death.

4

———

The air was full of fire and ash.

I walked towards the Sanctum, my hand curled tightly around my arondight hilt, Darkness invading my senses. It writhed around the ruined building like a disease, sucking the marrow out of ravaged bones like parasites. To my eyes, it was a giant storm cloud sparking with crimson bolts of lightning —the aura of pure evil.

The entryway was blown apart and the doors were hanging off their hinges. I stepped over the rubble and looked up at the statue of the Lady of the Lake, but it wasn't there anymore. Pieces of it lay down the stairs, the base a mass of jagged marble.

It was oddly quiet—the faint crackle of flames echoed from deeper within the building, but there was no other movement. As soon as I had entered the building, it was as if the demons had ceased their rampage and were waiting to see what I'd do.

My boots crunched on stone and glass, the sound

echoing in the stillness. Where were they? I could sense them lingering, watching and waiting…

"Come out, come out…" I whispered.

As if of on cue, lesser demons swarmed from the halls and skittered down the marble stairs towards me. I stood my ground, unafraid of the horde baring down on me. If I was going to prove to myself that I was capable of all the things the Lady of the Lake believed I could do, now was the time to prove it—to myself, to the Naturals who were waiting outside, and to those who had lost their lives here and around the world.

I wondered what Wilder would do right about now, but he wasn't here. Neither was Galahad, who'd been with me through my trials in the past. I had to stand on my own two feet as Arondight.

In less than a second, I took stock of all the holes the filth scurried out of and readied myself. *Game on, bitches.*

I brought my sword to life as the first rotting demon set foot in the foyer. Indigo sparks hissed as they scattered across the floor and I struck.

I cut through sagging flesh, sliced through brittle bone, and pirouetted so I could strike down another wave. My Light flared and I surrendered to the flame inside me, letting my instincts take control. Logic had no place here—I was a wild thing fighting against those who would rise up and harm me.

Was this what it was to be Arondight? All sense, feeling, and rage. Just rage.

I was surrounded by a pile of rotting corpses, my

sword dripping with congealed black blood. Shuddering, I flicked the blade and my Light seared the metal clean.

The next wave appeared, their boots thudding across the floor and trampling the demons I'd just cut down.

I froze. They were wearing black tactical gear and held arondight blades in their hands.

No…

They were Naturals. People who I'd trained with. People who I'd fought beside. People who I'd shared lunch with. My brothers and sisters, each one of them possessed.

Please…don't make me do it…

They came at me, their arondight blades sparking. I blocked a blow to my left, then to my right. Twisting, I kicked away a man to my rear.

"Stop it!" I shrieked at them. "Fight them!"

My blade clashed against a strike to my front, then I ducked a slash and kicked the legs out from underneath a woman who I remembered passing in the hall just this morning.

"You're possessed! Fight back!"

I slammed my elbow into the stomach, then rapped the flat of my sword hit against the temple of another man, sending him sprawling.

I cried out, rising to my feet and clashing with a savage blow from above. My eyes met the woman's and I froze.

Romy…

We stood eye to eye, our swords locked. Whatever

had taken hold of her had turned her cold. This wasn't Romy anymore. She was trapped inside her body and at the mercy of the Infernal who held her.

"Fight," I hissed. "You're stronger than they are. I believe in you, Romy."

Her lip curled and steel slid against steel and our deadlock broke. I twisted, bringing up my blade as she brought hers down. We clashed, locking against one another.

"It's over," she snarled, her voice twisted by the creature inside her. "We have them now. The rest will soon follow."

"No, you don't." I levelled my gaze with hers, knowing it was the possession talking. "You'll never get your hands on the Codex, and you will give up your hold on my friends."

She leaned her weight into her sword, baring down on me, then her expression began to fade.

"You can sense it, can't you?" I asked the creature inside her. "You know who I am."

Who, not what—that's where I'd been going wrong all this time. I'd believed Arondight was an ability, a power to be manipulated, but as I stood here, locked in a battle of wills with one of my best friends, I knew I'd been looking at it from the wrong angle. *I was Arondight*. It was my identity, my soul.

I let my hold on my sword slip and went down onto my knees as Romy's blade lowered towards my neck.

I was Arondight.

I let go of the hilt and slammed my hand against

her stomach and pushed my Light outwards. A burst of indigo flame lit her from the inside, a shockwave of energy pulsing through the room. The circle of possessed Naturals fell like dominos, their blades clattering to the marble floor.

She fell against me and I propped her up, easing her to her knees. She blinked, her eyes regaining some of their warmth. Colour was flushing her cheeks as the others began to stir. The Infernals were gone and whatever infection they carried had disappeared with them.

"Romy?" I smoothed my hands over her face and checked her temperature like it was supposed to do something. After what I'd just done, it was strange to think I was totally winging it when it came to aftercare.

"It…evaporated." She stared at me in awe. "The Infernal just—"

"You need to get out of here," I told her. "Take them and find Aldrich. They were headed towards Westminster."

She nodded. "I know where he's headed, but what about you?"

"I have to get the Codex."

"But—"

"I'll be fine." I pulled her in for a hug. "*Please. Go now.*"

"We can't… We… The Sanctum—"

I pulled back. "Romy. The Sanctum is lost. We need to gather our strength elsewhere." I nodded towards the door. "Go."

She inclined her head and I helped her to her feet. As the Naturals gathered their strength and began to leave in search of Aldrich and Greer, I turned to the stairs.

As my boot touched the first step, my stomach flip-flopped. The demons had given up their hold on Human Convergence so easily, which meant whatever had attacked the Sanctum was far worse than any mutation we had come across. I doubted it was the Dark's trump card, but it was the storm before the atomic bomb.

Long story short, whatever it was, it was bad news.

The stench of sulphur and brimstone filled the air as I reached the upper floor. I walked through the Sanctum, my arondight blade dragging against the ground, my anger boiling over.

The displays of weapons I'd always admired were nothing but twisted and melted metal. The paintings of famous Naturals which hung proudly in dedicated alcoves were slashed and torn. Priceless tapestries were burned, and statues and iconography dedicated to the Lady of the Lake had been disfigured and desecrated.

We were being erased.

Demons lingered in the shadows as I passed, hissing and spitting, none brave enough to stand before me. They knew what I'd done and could sense the power in me—*cowards*. They were just foot soldiers, and Wilder had called them cannon fodder— they were nothing more than expendable husks that crowded around the feet of their master.

Whoever had led the assault was ahead, trying to pry the Codex out of its protective shell. That's where the real battle would lie.

I climbed the stairs to the conservatory, my boots light on the wrought iron. I wasn't afraid, there was no room for it. I sheathed my sword, knowing it was only an extension of what I could do on my own.

As I reached the landing, I finally saw it, its towering bulk pure Darkness. The oppressive presence I'd felt since entering the Sanctum stood in the centre of the conservatory, looming over the Codex. As it turned, flame hissed as it left smouldering ash in its wake. Black essence shimmered around it as two red eyes met my gaze, its face a ruin of twisted flesh and bone.

It wasn't a greater demon like Markzoth—it was something else, something *more*.

I stood my ground as the horror show moved towards me, its body morphing with every step. More human features began to emerge from the nightmarish construct—the sharp line of a jaw, angled cheekbones, muscled arms, and ivory flesh made new.

It was a man within a creature, a shapeshifter.

"You alone?" His voice was a rasp as if his monstrous essence had shredded his throat. More of his true body appeared, and he was clad in leather and steel armour which reminded me of an age long past—the age of Camelot.

A wave of nausea threatened to topple me as the sound of his words reached my ears. Whatever he was, he was as powerful as the final stroke of death itself, but I held strong.

"Me alone," I told him, dancing at the Codex. *He couldn't get into the enclosure.*

"Who are you to challenge me?"

I narrowed my eyes, the indigo flame simmering inside my heart. "Who are you to stand before me, in my house, and demand anything?"

"I am Mordred," he snarled. "I am not them and I am not you...*Natural.*"

Mordred... I knew his name from the human stories—he was Arthur's bastard son, but in reality, he could be anyone. If I took the guy at face value, he was the enemy.

"My mother looked at me like that in the end," he said, towering over me. "Like I was evil incarnate."

"Your mother?"

"Think about it. Think really hard." His lip curled as his boot crunched on the broken glass of the dome. "I want you to know before you die."

I stared at him in horror as I realised the depth of what was wrought the night Camelot was torn apart.

Guinevere. The demons had taken her the night of the cataclysm and used her in their experiments. Everything they'd done—every breakthrough, every mutation—had been at her expense.

Mordred was the first subject of Human Convergence. Born of Guinevere and...and who? The One?

"No," I whispered, shaking my head. "You were the beginning."

"They call me the harbinger," his lips curved upwards in a triumphant smirk, "*of death*."

Everything we were was stripped bare and exposed. The Naturals were nothing. We'd ruined ourselves. We'd ruined this world. Everything that'd happened was our fault. We'd practically handed this world to the demons on a silver platter.

"*Yes*," he hissed, his mind baring down on mine, "you invited us in."

He was stronger than anything I'd ever faced, but I was Arondight. I was the greatest hope for the Naturals and this world. I could lay here and let Mordred take my power and drive the final nail into the coffin, or I could fight back and create a new future.

Mordred was twisted, but his heart was still human—I could feel it beat inside his chest. Arondight knew and so did I. There was Light there, but there was no doubt in my mind that it was irredeemable.

"You know." He grasped my face and twisted it to the side, his gaze raking over my scar. "How do you know?" He wasn't talking about his mother anymore. Could he sense my thoughts? Was that what he was doing?

"I know more than you ever will," I snarled. "I come from a place beyond your comprehension, *demon*."

It was his turn to stare at me in disbelief. "*Arondight*."

I smirked and lifted a brow. "Surprise, arsehole."

A pulse of indigo flame exploded from within me, the blast throwing Mordred backwards. He let me go, crying out in pure rage as I tore my arondight blade out of my belt and brought it to life. The sword clicked into place, showering the conservatory with sparks, and I swung.

Mordred recovered quickly, drawing his own blade, and our weapons crashed together with a force that jarred up both of my arms and rattled my teeth.

We stood within an inch of each other, and Mordred snarled at me, his eyes cold and dark. Whatever good he'd been born with had been twisted beyond recognition. The spark of Light I'd sensed was so far from his grasp, it was hopeless. It tormented him—I could feel it in his aura.

Our swords slid against one other and we broke apart, indigo sparks mixing with crimson. What was it with pure evil and the colour red? Blood gave life, didn't it? Who knew, because I had no idea why I was so purple about stuff.

I twisted, blocking a strike, then returned fire. I leapt, pushing off the floor with a burst of Light, and swung at Mordred's neck, but he phased in and out of reality in a burst of swirling blackness.

I faltered, surprised by the sudden change in reality and it gave him an opening.

He struck me with the flat of his blade and the coppery tang of blood exploded across my tongue. The force of the blow pushed me to my knees, and I landed hard, gasping for breath. A wave of pure

Darkness passed through me, twisting my heart and I cried out as I was kicked to the floor.

My cheek pressed against the rubble from the dome, my flesh stinging as shards of glass sliced into my skin.

"You are nothing," Mordred snarled, grinding his boot into my spine. "Without Excalibur, you cannot defeat me."

I cried out in pain, the taste of blood thick on my tongue. He was right... I didn't stand a chance against him. For all the power I held, his Darkness was more.

"You're *pathetic*."

Maybe I was, but for all his Darkness, I pitied the man he'd become. His life had been taken away from him before he'd been even born, and there was no redemption waiting for Mordred...only death.

"What... would... your... mother... think?" I rasped, my gaze finding the Codex.

"I wouldn't know. *I killed her*."

In that moment, as the pain of what he'd done burned into my heart, I let go. Indigo flame exploded out of me, throwing Mordred across the room.

Suddenly, I was free.

Pushing to my feet, I hurled myself at the enclosure in the centre of the room, my shoulder smashing through the glass. The jagged pieces tore open my flesh, but I ignored the pain and snatched the Codex.

Mordred let out an unholy scream and the room filled with flame that pulsed with demonic souls. They flew around me, tearing at my arms, tugging my hair, and trying to push me over. I struggled against them, shielding the book, but as fingers grasped at the cover, they burst into flame, the protective spells searing the spirits from the inside out.

Mordred roared from somewhere behind me as I found the edge of the building where the wall had been smashed open. The city stretched before me and a twisted pile of steel and rock lay five stories below.

I looked at the carnage and felt the pull of utter desolation behind me and knew this was only the beginning. The death and destruction was only a drop compared to the desolation that waited on the other side of the rift.

The end times were upon us.

I grasped the Codex against my chest and jumped.

5

I didn't land.
  I flew.
I floated.
I sank.

Water enveloped me, dragging me down to the inky black depths. Ice bled into my veins, rushing through my limbs and into my heart. I raised my hand, searching for the surface, but it was far above and out of reach. *Too far.*

I blinked, my lungs screaming for air and kicked.

Scarlett.

A woman reached for me from above, her pale hand like a ghostly apparition in the inky depths. Her dress billowed in the water, her hair shimmering like starlight as it fanned around her serene face. She smiled, her hand reaching for mine.

The Lady of the Lake.

Our fingers grazed the other and her warmth spread into me.

Come, Scarlett. It's not your time.

Was she real or simply a figment of my oxygen-starved brain? I thought she'd passed into memory, leaving our world with the Druids beyond the portals of Avalon.

I took her hand and water rushed past in a shower of bubbles, then the world opened up to me. Air brushed against my skin and an unbearable pressure in my chest jerked me into reality.

I gasped for breath as awareness returned, and I choked. Rolling onto my side, I coughed up gross-tasting water, spitting onto a shore of rocks and pebbles. The shore of what? I always seemed to be dumped in water and it was getting real old, real fast.

"Scarlett!" Hands patted me on the back, and I flung my arm out wildly, only to come face to face with Jackson.

I blinked furiously and shivered. "*The Codex.* Where's the Codex?"

"We've got it." He grasped me tightly in an attempt to reassure me. "*We've got it.*"

"You can't—"

"Touch it?" he interrupted. "Yeah, we know."

I looked to the side, finding Esme kneeling beside us holding something wrapped in Jackson's coat. *The Codex.*

"My arondight blade." My heart leapt and I patted my belt. Finding no trace of the hilt, I began to feel along the pebbled shore around me.

"It's not here," Jackson said. "You must have dropped it."

"No…"

"You can get another one," he said in an attempt to calm me.

"You don't understand," I wailed. "It's the only thing I have left of my mother." I'd lost everything—Andromeda's sword, Galahad's note, and Wilder's troll doll. If I wanted to be selfish and save something sentimental from a burning building, it would have been those three things.

I let out a cry and rubbed my stinging arms. My back ached from Mordred's boot and his power had left an uncomfortable tightness in my mind.

What had happened to the others… Alo, Martin, and Valeria? Aiden hadn't returned to the Academy yet—he'd been inside the Sanctum. Oh God, the Academy! There were almost a hundred students and teachers. Had Islington and Adelaide gotten them out in time, or was it still standing? Ramona and Madeleine were also unaccounted for, and I couldn't hold on to my anguish anymore.

I sobbed, my fingers digging into the stony shore. I was supposed to save them all and now, they could all be dead.

"She's in shock, Jackson," Esme murmured, kneeling beside me. "We have to get her someplace warm."

He hesitated, then looked at me. "The safe house."

Esme looked between us. "What safe house?"

"After Scarlett and Wilder broke me out of the Sanctum when I was going to be executed—"

"Wait…you were going to be executed?"

I looked across the water at the smoking ruin of the Sanctum and sensed the Darkness swirling through the flames. Mordred was up there and soon the city would be swarming with demons looking for me and the Codex…and every last Natural.

I wiped my eyes and took a couple of deep breaths. The water smelt like mouldy weeds and had soaked me through, but I had to keep going. Wilder was still alive, and he was in trouble. Without him, the Naturals had nothing; but if he was lost, I… I loved him. If Wilder was no more, I wouldn't know what to do.

"Scarlett?"

I looked up at Jackson and Esme. We had to get off the streets but getting off the shores of the Thames would be a good start.

"We need to go," I said, pushing to my feet. I grimaced as a dull throbbing ache bloomed through my lower back. "It's not safe out here."

We climbed up the embankment and onto the footpath, my feet squelching in my boots. Esme offered me her jacket, but I shook my head, telling her that I could use a little Light to help speed up the drying process.

I kept catching myself using my abilities sparingly as if my time with Galahad had ingrained the importance of remaining hidden. Of course, the demons couldn't track us like they used to, but using Light as little as possible was also something Wilder had taught me.

The three of us ghosted through the streets, weaving a path through the city away from the Sanctum and the ever-increasing demonic presence. Esme grasped the wrapped-up Codex close to her chest, Jackson brought up the rear, and I took the lead. Without my arondight blade or my cold iron dagger, I felt naked.

"It's strange…" Esme mused as we found a main thoroughfare lit by bright streetlamps. "There's all this destruction and to the humans, it's like nothing has happened."

"It's a thankless job," I drawled as a group of humans passed.

They were all huddled deep within their coats and scarfs, earphones stuck in their ears, and smartphones glued to their noses. A war was raging in their city and they were completely oblivious. We wanted it that way, but the contrast was jarring after the night we had.

Flagging down a taxi, I glanced over my shoulder. The street was clear behind us, but it wouldn't be for long. Soon, even innocent humans would be used against us and there would be nowhere to turn.

Time was running out.

***

The safe house was just as I remembered it.

Now my senses were completely open to the world, I could see the house Wilder had so painstakingly cloaked.

The two-story row house looked like it should be condemned. It sat tacked onto the end of a well-kept streetscape with an empty lot on the other side. The tiny garden was overgrown, and grass sprouted from between the cracks in the footpath. Yellow and grey splotches of lichen grew over the steps and onto the rotting façade, the wood that had once been painted white was now split and crumbling from decades of disrepair. It seemed the only thing holding this place together was the illusion which concealed it from the world.

Wilder had never really explained why he'd felt the need to have a haven. *Not really*. Always branded as an outsider—even though he was Natural through and through—he believed he needed a place that was sealed away from the world he'd strived to save…and master. Had some part of him known the truth of who he was all along? It was difficult to say.

Inside, the house smelt musty as if it'd been closed up for a long time. No one had been here in months and my heart sank. It was wishful thinking to hope that Wilder was here, but wished I had.

I ran my fingers over the peeling wallpaper and stared up the crooked stairs. The floorboards were warped, which made the floor look like waves in the ocean, and treacherous for the newly initiated. Jackson guided Esme into the front room, flicking the light switch as he went.

She still had the Codex and I was glad to let her take custodianship of it for the time being. We had no way of getting in contact with the others, and I wasn't sure where Aldrich had led them.

The logical thing to do would be to use my abilities, but the harder I reached, the farther away they seemed to be. Facing Mordred like that… The reality of who he was and what he'd become weighed heavily on me.

We'd let them in.

I found my way into the front room—where the mattress from our last stay was still on the floor—and leaned against the wall by the front window. Easing the blind away from the wall, I peered out onto the darkened street. It was deathly silent, which only unnerved me more.

"There should be stuff in the kitchen," Jackson said, "and spare clothes in the bedroom down the hall."

"I'll get something together for dinner," Esme told us. "Food will make us all feel better, right?"

I didn't think anything would make me feel better, but I let her fuss because it made her heart lighter.

She ventured down the hall like a woman on a mission, leaving me and Jackson alone in the front room. How do I tell them about Mordred and the truth of who and what he represented? I hoped the Naturals I'd fought had made it out safely and had found Aldrich and Greer.

"The cupboards are full of food," I heard Esme exclaim from the kitchen. "There's at least twenty cans of dinosaur-shaped spaghetti."

Jackson looked at me, a smile on his lips. "I remember those dinosaurs fondly."

I didn't have it in me to smile, so I turned back to the window as if Wilder would appear at any second.

"How did you find me?" I asked.

"We could sense you and whatever that thing was in the conservatory," he replied. "We left the others with Aldrich and came to find you. I figured you needed some help getting out of there, but when you jumped—"

I turned. "You saw me jump?"

"Scarlett…you flew."

I blinked. It was a blur from the time I'd jumped to the moment I'd woken up on the shore of the Thames. "I… I don't remember."

He frowned but didn't say anything else. Things had gotten crazier by the second and even attempting to understand the unexplainable was so far out of reach it wasn't even funny.

"Didn't the demons try to follow you?" I asked.

"They didn't seem interested in us…probably because of our mutations."

I nodded and wrapped my arms around my middle.

"You should take a shower," he said. "Warm yourself up. Esme will be awhile."

"Jackson…" I was lost for words. The struggle was real, as was the horror that'd unfolded across the world only hours ago.

"I know, Scarlett," he said. "I'm afraid, too."

"I don't know what I'm supposed to do. All these people are counting on me and—"

He placed his hands on my shoulders. "We'll figure it out, Scarlett. We always do."

"How did we get here?" I whispered, my bottom lip trembling. It seemed like so long ago that I'd been a mediocre woman standing behind the bar at *8-bit* agonising over my meds and Jackson was gearing up to compete in the latest e-sports tournament at the *O2 Arena* in Greenwich.

But now… Now, I held the fate of the world in my hands.

"That's the crazy thing," he replied. "I don't think anyone knows how they end up anywhere."

"Yeah." I shivered and looked towards the window.

"C'mon," he said, gathering me in his arms, "let's clean up, have something to eat, get some rest, then regroup. We'll make a plan, but we're safe. I promise."

Jackson trusted Wilder. That was a first.

I found some spare clothes in the bedroom down the hall. They were too big for me being Wilder-sized, but it was better than nothing.

The bathroom was just as tiny and full of mould as I remembered. The walls were pink and the pipes were covered in rust, but the water was warm and there was soap. I'd been here before and I shivered at the memory of Wilder kneeling before me, cleaning the blood off my hands after I'd healed Jackson.

Steam filled the tiny space and I found my

thoughts wandering as the ache began to fade from my limbs.

The cuts and scratches from where I'd smashed through the glass surrounding the Codex had disappeared completely, but the places Mordred had struck—my face and back—still throbbed. What was with that?

I'd say I was surprised, but nothing about my reality surprised me anymore.

Water pounded against my back and I rubbed the soap over my arms.

Sanctums all over the world had fallen. The desolation in London was only one site of many. Hundreds of Naturals had likely been possessed or killed. We had been too few and now we were not enough. We had finally reached the brink and the abyss waited just beyond.

Our only hope lay with Arondight uniting with Excalibur.

Wilder with his silver eyes and surly attitude. The Argent Flame.

Wilder.

I breathed deeply, the scent of the soap filling my senses to the brim—it smelt like him.

"Where are you…?" I whispered, longing for his touch.

He was gone, but he was in everything around me.

Where are you? Where are you? Where are you?

He was everywhere and nowhere.

6

———

I couldn't sleep.

My mind kept turning over and over, worrying about my friends, the other Naturals around the world, and Mordred.

Maybe I should be reading the Codex so I could learn from battles long past, but I couldn't bring myself to even do that. Instead, I wandered the house, trying to find any clues Wilder may have left behind.

I wasn't surprised when I found a cache of weapons hidden in a secret crawlspace in the basement. It wouldn't be a safe house with Wilder's stamp of approval if there wasn't a significant arsenal squirrelled away some place. The dinosaur spaghetti and the closet of fitted black T-shirts didn't count.

It was dank and dark down here, but I found a light hanging from the ceiling and pulled the little cord to turn it on. It clicked, illuminating the space in a muted glow. A boiler sat on one side amongst a pile of junk that must have lived upstairs at one time or another, and cobwebs draped thickly in the corners.

Catching my reflection in an old mirror with a rusted back, I paused. My hair had only become more purple in the aftermath of my awakening, but my eyes were still the same chocolate brown I shared with my mother. I looked older somehow, as if the past year had aged me into a whole new decade.

I was twenty-six. I'd missed my birthday somewhere in the past eight hundred years, but it didn't seem to matter—age was now completely irrelevant.

I dragged the black hard case I'd found hidden in the wall into a clear space on the floor and promptly undid the latches. As expected, it was full of daggers, knives, throwing blades, and a spare arondight hilt. I snatched up the latter with greedy fingers and inspected it in minute detail.

It was made for a heavier hand—like Wilder's— and the hilt was a little too long for me to grip comfortably. The design was sleek and modern, likely a newer sword which wouldn't be missed if someone pilfered it from a certain armoury. Granted, it wasn't Andromeda's, but it was better than nothing.

The sound of light footsteps on the rickety stairs drew my attention and I slipped the hilt into my coat pocket.

Esme appeared feet first, then her head ducked down as she descended into the basement. "There you are. I was wondering where you'd disappeared to."

"I couldn't sleep," I said, holding up a cold iron dagger. I inspected the edge and put it in a newly formed 'yes' pile.

"No, I suppose not."

I sat on the dirty floor and continued to pull out treasure after treasure from the case.

"You found some weapons?" she asked, sitting beside me.

"Wilder hid them in the wall." I narrowed my eyes, wanting nothing more than to be alone.

"Oh…"

I held onto a sigh. "Where's Jackson? Has something happened?"

"Oh, nothing like that," Esme replied. "I just wanted to make sure you were okay."

I shrugged.

"Are you?" She looked at me hopefully. Man, her eyes were so big it was no wonder Jackson fawned over her. "I mean, after what you went through to get the Codex back… Well, I can't imagine what you had to face up there. You almost drowned in the Thames, Scarlett, and here you are only hours later, getting ready for the next fight. And you haven't slept!"

She was trying to reach out to me in her own awkward, rambling way, not as Arondight, but as Scarlett Ravenwood, aka Jackson's best friend. Even now, in the aftermath of such destruction, she didn't see me as a weapon, but as a person.

I shook my head. "How can I sleep when my friends are dying and the man I love is missing?"

Her expression softened as she picked up a cold iron dagger.

"Have you trained any?" I asked, watching her closely.

"A little. I'm just the support staff as you know, so I just got the basics."

She held the dagger like it was a foreign object and I wondered how she'd gotten through the fight at the alpha site. I hadn't really been paying attention.

"What did you do before?"

Her eyes widened. "Before?"

"Before you joined the Sanctum."

Esme's lips thinned as she put the dagger back inside the case.

"You weren't a stripper, were you?" I asked.

"No! Nothing like that," she spluttered.

I raised my eyebrows.

She shook her head. "No, it's stupid."

"Tell me."

She glanced at me, her cheeks heating. It totally sucked being pale—every little flush was a major affair.

"I was a nobody before..." she told me, "a coaster."

I tilted my head to the side. "A coaster?"

"I didn't really know who I wanted to be, so I floated from job to job and moved around a lot." Her eyes widened as I pulled out a knife with a savage serrated edge. "Since...since I joined the Sanctum, I have a place. I feel awful for even saying this, but—"

"Being infected was the best thing that ever happened to you?"

Her chin lifted and her gaze met mine. She flushed again, this time a deeper shade than before.

"Don't worry about it," I added. "we're all a little weird around here."

We fell into a companionable silence as I stashed a dagger I wanted to keep in my boot and shoved the rest back into the case.

"So…" Esme dusted off her trousers, "did I pass the test?"

I snorted. She wanted my approval to date Jackson? It seemed outlandish that she'd even think she needed to ask.

"We don't administer those kinds of tests around here," I told her.

She laughed and shook her head. "Good. I was worried."

"I just want him to be happy and safe." I made a face and rose to my feet. "I'm currently working on both those things."

Esme followed suit and stared up at me, her slight form humming with a bright orange glow. Tiny sparks of red zapped here and there, a telltale sign of her mutation.

My abilities were coming back, and I was beginning to think it had something to do with my state of mind. The Lady of the Lake had been so serene, I wondered if the way Arondight had merged with my soul was on more of a spiritual level than physical. It made sense considering I'd always been so instinctive about things. Knowing it would be a great help and hanging out here trying to think of a way to combat the current state of affairs wasn't an optimal use of my time.

"I need to do something, and I know Jackson isn't going to like it," I declared.

Esme hesitated. "Uh oh…"

"I have to go out into the city and search for Wilder. *Alone.*" If I was solo, I'd have a clear head to hone my abilities.

"But we have no leads," she argued. "You'd be going out there blind, and the whole city is crawling with demonic activity."

I looked at her and wondered what a bright pumpkin orange aura meant. I detected a little yellow here and there, especially around her head. It was a specific colour if you asked me.

"I won't find him hiding out here," I told her.

"What about the Codex?"

"It'll be safe in the house."

"What about me and Jackson? We have demonic DNA. We can fly under the radar."

"You just said you've only had basic combat training. You've both got your strengths, but can you perform an exorcism to save an innocent? Can you bring yourself to cut down a rotting corpse? Can you face a greater demon?"

She blinked and shook her head, her expression falling.

"I'm not trying to be mean, Esme," I murmured, "I'm trying to protect you." I drew in a shaky breath and looked into the rusty mirror. "We've already lost so much. I-I can't lose anymore."

I tensed as she placed a hand on my arm.

"You'll find him," she said. "I know you will."

I nodded. "Help me sneak out of the house?" We both knew Jackson had the hearing *and eyes* of a hawk these days. He'd become a helicopter parent since I'd returned from the past.

"Sure," she replied with a smile. "I've got the perfect way to distract him."

I smirked and wiggled my eyebrows. "Oh, I bet you do."

Night swirled around London like an old friend.

I sat on a ledge beside the Thames, watching a variety of boats going to and fro underneath Tower Bridge. It was a world-famous tourist icon and I could see people lingering on the banks of the Thames taking photographs of the lit-up structure. I snorted as I saw a couple attempting to take a creative selfie and wondered what hashtag they'd use.

I'd found a hoodie that'd belonged to Wilder and huddled into it. It was too large, but it was warm and the hood pulled all the way up over my head, concealing my hair and face from the world. With my leather jacket over the top, it kept out most of the chill of the fast-approaching winter.

Where would he go? I shook my head. That

wasn't right. He disappeared looking for me, so where did he think I would go to look for Arondight?

He'd assisted in the search of the Academy grounds, and when they'd found no trace, he'd returned to London for some unknown reason and resumed his crusade here. But why? The trail would've turned up cold at the standing stones, so it made no sense. Had his bound abilities as Excalibur unconsciously told him something only I could figure out?

Whatever it was, something had led him back here, but I had no idea what it might be. There'd been no indication in the reports he'd left after returning, but it *was* Wilder I was attempting to track. He had a knack for blowing off the authorities and leaving no trace. Still, something told me he was close, just out of reach, waiting for me.

I wasn't in the position to ignore my gut feeling, so I left Tower Bridge and its tourists behind and wandered the city, allowing my power to soar. Arondight called out for its twin flame, so if anyone could find him, it was me—I just had to lose myself in the stars.

I was beginning to accept my identity and what had once overwhelmed—the swirling mass of auras in a city overflowing with life—was now becoming normal.

I'd wandered all the way to Covent Garden before I realised it. Cloaked and silent, I'd woven a path back to familiar ground, somehow avoiding all traces of demonic energy. If I opened myself enough, I could feel the Darkness all around, pulsating like a blight on the city. The balance had finally tipped.

In the market, a busker was belting out a cover of *The Smiths'* 'There Is a Light That Never Goes Out' on an acoustic guitar, his voice amplified as he sung into a battered microphone. I paused, listening to the emo lyrics. *The Smiths* really sung about some depressing shite—the melancholy of a generation.

It wasn't until I'd stopped that I could sense *them* lingering in the shadows, leaping amongst human bodies trying to keep me within their sights. I was the ultimate prize, a gift to be laid triumphantly at their master's feet. They were leaving me be for now, waiting to see what I'd do or who I'd lead them to. Narrowing my eyes, I watched the busker as he moved onto another song.

When his gaze found mine, I wasn't surprised. I was cloaked, but with a demon inside the poor guy he could see right through the glamour.

They were taunting me, letting me know they held all the power. I was nothing without my Twin Flame. Well, I had news for them—I mightn't have Wilder by my side, but I still packed a pretty solo punch.

Snarling, I stepped towards the busker, narrowly avoiding slamming into the steam of humans strolling through the market. My cloak extended, dissolving the both of us into invisibility, and I fisted my hand into the guy's minimalist grey T-shirt. Wrenching him close, the movement knocked over his microphone stand and it fell to the ground with a clatter. The sound drew the attention of passersby, but they didn't see us.

"You think you're so smart," I hissed. "You think you've won? You think you can follow me and I won't know about it?"

"We have the power now," the demon rasped, its voice shredding the busker's throat. "You're kind is on the path of extinction."

"*We'll see about that.*"

"You think your flame can save them? *Look around.*"

I hissed and tore my gaze away from his black eyes. Looking around the market, I realised the noise of the nighttime shoppers had died away and we were standing in a bubble of hushed silence—unusual for a city crammed to the brim with people.

A sea of Darkness stared back at me and my grip loosened on the busker. The crowd circled us, each one of them full with demonic entities—Infernals and other creatures I hadn't even knew existed. Mordred had really pulled out all the stops.

Their eyes stared at me, black and evil. I was screwed, but I had an ace up my sleeve.

"They're innocents," I spat. "How do you live with yourselves?"

"They exist to be consumed. Life is to be inhabited." The busker/demon curled his lip and laughed. "Humans are just like us. They multiply like locusts and strip the world bare...and you want to save them?"

"Unlike you, we have remorse for what we've done."

"Do you? I'm fairly sure this body I inhabit doesn't care."

I let out a cry of anger and grabbed him around the throat. "This isn't open for discussion. Get. Out. Of. *Him*."

A burst of indigo flame pulsed into his body and I felt the Infernal bristle and boil away. Anger pulsed in my heart and I ignited, my Light blasting out through the barrier of demons around us.

The shockwave tore through the market with incredible force, the explosion tearing through everything around me.

Gasping, I let the busker go and he fell to the ground unconscious.

The footpath was blown to pieces and the widows of the surrounding shops were shattered. Stalls which lined the cobbled paths were little more than matchsticks, and here I stood in the centre of the blast radius.

I covered my mouth with my hand as I stared at the humans lying on the ground. They were covered in soot, broken glass, and splotches of blood. Turning, I could sense they were all alive and the demons were dead, but they so easily could've followed the parasites into the abyss.

Sirens wailed and people rushed from other parts of the market to assist the injured. They couldn't see me, but I could see what I'd done. What had I done? I was utter desolation.

I'd used Arondight with anger in my heart and now I understood the importance of love. This was what had torn Camelot apart and opened the rift.

Choking back a sob, I fled into the night.

<hr>

I ran away. I knew those people would be okay, but I was terrified of the destruction within me. Merged with Excalibur, we could tear apart not just a footpath, but the *entire world*.

Wiping at my eyes, I stilled my flight and looked around. I'd lost the demons on my tail and had found myself at a familiar crossroad—Seven Dials.

The tiny and confusing roundabout was full of utter chaos. Cars attempted to navigate the intersection as people crossed the street in a wild game of chicken.

Seven obscure passages. Seven different roads. A place for the less fortunate to find their fate.

I couldn't stay here, so I chose the most familiar path and took a sharp right.

I put my head down as I walked down the alley, the cobblestones slick underfoot. It was only wide enough for two people to walk abreast, and I found myself dodging from side to side to avoid colliding with unsuspecting humans.

The buildings towered over me, rising two to three stories above. The same array of boutique shops lit the narrow street with cheery warm light and the scents of food, coffee, and overly scented skin care products filled the air.

As I emerged into the courtyard, I scanned the nighttime revellers as they milled about the shops and cafés. Overhead, strings of fairy lights gave a festive feel to the little alcove and the looming holiday season sent a pang ricocheting through my heart.

Music pumped out of the pub on the corner and people milled about the array of folding chairs and tables as they ignored the chill in favour of the atmosphere. I was reminded of the *Hung, Drawn and Quartered* near Tower Hill where Wilder liked to drown his sorrows, the perfume of old beer bringing our earliest confrontations to mind.

Though I didn't like the crowd—knowing there was an army of demons scouring the city—I lingered. The first time Wilder brought me here, this whole space had been protected from the Dark, but after I'd come back… Well, we all knew how that had ended.

I looked up at the place Gilhana's ramshackle house had once stood, concealed between the skincare shop and the vegan bakery. It was long gone, the city had swallowed it up with her death, but the more I thought about it, the more I realised it'd never existed. I'd completed the druidess's prism, so her future here hadn't come to pass. She'd been erased and any clue she might've left wouldn't even be a thing.

I was alone.

My chest tightened and I sidled up to a table outside the pub. A man set down a round of pints he'd just bought for his friends. When they weren't looking, I pilfered one of the beers and found a quiet place where the patronage wouldn't bump into the invisible hybrid from another world.

I sipped the alcohol, feeling like a total fraud. The headlines in tomorrow's newspapers would talk of a terrorist attack, that I was sure of. The police would shut down the markets and do their forensic investigation. They'd see an innocent busker dissolve from reality, then the queerest sight they'd ever see in their lives—a circle of people standing around an empty space, then *boom*. If there wasn't a supernatural Taskforce in place, there would be one now. Without a team of Naturals to clean up my mess, humanity would soon become aware that they weren't alone.

As I watched the surrounding hubbub, I took another sip of the stolen beer. Not one of them showed signs of demonic possession and I wasn't about to draw attention to myself looking for trouble.

As the hour grew late, the humans began to leave one by one. The shops closed, followed by the cafés, whose workers dragged tables and chairs inside. Finally, the pub pulled up stumps and the lights turned off. The ghostly fingers of thick frost began to creep into the courtyard, chilling everything it touched.

I didn't know what to do. Wilder wasn't here and he'd always been here. Someone had almost always helped me stand up to the bad guys, but now I was completely on my own and I was failing miserably.

Closing my eyes, I leaned against the wall of the pub and breathed deeply, my lungs filling with ice. I couldn't feel the cold anymore—I'd become numb to it.

I dropped my guard and that's when I felt it. *Darkness.*

My eyes flew open and fixed on a man standing in the centre of the courtyard. He was staring at me, his stature solid and well-built.

"Wilder?" I whispered.

Blinking, I looked at him again and realised it was something else. Reaching for the arondight blade in my coat pocket, I pulled it out. The metal was unfamiliar in my hand as I stepped forwards, knowing one of Mordred's minions was making a play for its prize.

An aura of death surrounded the greater demon, all sparks.

"That was an impressive show of power," he declared, stepping out of the shadows. "I haven't seen the like of it since you tore apart Camelot."

"That wasn't me," I snarled, looking over the hack job it'd done on its pieced-together body. Whoever this was, he didn't have the same flair with a sewing machine as Markzoth.

"Careful," the demon warned, "you don't want to face me with anger, Arondight. You know what will happen if you do."

"Eat shite."

He bared his teeth—rows upon rows of sharp points—and strode towards me. "Keep her alive, he said. We need the flame to open the way."

"I'd rather *die*," I hissed, slamming my hands onto

his face. The demon screamed as his flesh boiled underneath my palms. The air filled with the stench of cooking flesh. "I killed Markzoth and I will kill you, too."

The demon began to laugh even as his grotesque construct of a body boiled under my touch. "Go ahead. I'll gladly walk into the abyss if it means blackening your fickle human heart."

"I'm not afraid of you, not anymore."

"You should be," he cried, his congealed blood bubbling out of his mouth like tar. "But you should be more afraid of yourself."

Indigo flame erupted out of me, pulsing through my hands and tearing apart the greater demon.

Then, the world exploded.

7

My ears were ringing. Rolling onto my side, I blinked my vision clear and I coughed up the dust that was clogging my lungs.

Sirens blared in the distance and I pushed to my knees, my palms pressing against my temples. My head buzzed with latent energy and the after-effects of being at ground zero of an explosion that'd torn the front off an entire circle of centuries old shops and houses.

I'd done this. This was my fault.

I sobbed, clawing at my head. I couldn't do it. I couldn't save the world. I had too much hate inside me. The Darkness had killed so many of my friends not even a day ago, and I was supposed to fight them with love in my heart? How in the world was I supposed to do that? It was impossible!

The loathing tore at my soul and I knew… Without Wilder, I wouldn't be able to see anything other than hate.

I had to turn it off. I had to let go of the Flame, otherwise I could wind up killing innocents and I'd never forgive myself. What would happen if I used my power with regret and self-loathing in my heart? I didn't want to know.

So, I shut off my link to Arondight…and the world went dark.

I was plain, old Scarlett Ravenwood again. The Scarlett I thought I was going to become the day I met the Lady of the Lake. I had my Light, but it felt like a mere sputtering spark compared to what I'd been with the Indigo Flame.

At least I wouldn't inadvertently hurt anyone.

I pushed to my feet and swayed as I picked across the rubble. The shop fronts had blown in, exposing their innards to the courtyard. I could smell the heady scent of expensive soaps and skin care products mixed with the charred burning, and the slight hiss of natural gas from a burst main somewhere. The headlines in tomorrow's papers had changed yet again. *Terrorist attack or gas leak?*

Turning, I looked down at the place where the greater demon had been standing. A scorch mark seared the ground and a ring of destruction fanned out around it—exactly where I'd stood and let go of my power.

I was right about the utter desolation.

The sound of sirens was becoming louder, so I made sure I was cloaked before making myself scarce. I took the alley to the north, passing by the remains of the vegan bakery. God, these people would come back to their businesses and be devastated by what they found was left behind. I'd left them with nothing. Guilt filled my heart and I quickened my step.

"Hey, Purples."

I came to an abrupt stop, pausing in the middle of the cobbled street. Looking up, my heart twisted when I saw a familiar form at the opposite end of the ally, silhouetted by the artificial glow of the city.

He stepped out of the shadows and his face came into view. He looked more rugged than usual, his jaw covered in way too much stubble and his hair was overgrown. It looked like he'd been through war.

"Wilder!" I ran towards him with tears of relief in my eyes. "I thought I'd lost you!"

I threw my arms around his neck and held him tight. Breathing in his scent, I clung to his shirt. When he didn't make a move to embrace me, I hesitated.

"Scarlett," he said, "it's so nice to see you again."

It's so nice to see you again? Wilder would never say something as bland as that.

I pulled back, my gaze searching his. Something wasn't right. There was no spark behind his eyes, no cheer, no cheek, no…

"Things must stay as they are." His expression twisted and he struck.

A sharp pain sliced through my stomach, making me double over with a cry. My eyes widened as I saw his hand curled around the hilt of a sword and it took a moment for the gravity of the situation to sink in.

His arondight blade impaled through my stomach, but I couldn't feel anything. Was this how shock worked? I knew I was in pain, but there was nothing to go along with it.

"Wilder?" I gasped. "*Why…?*"

He twisted the sword and the blade tore through my internal organs. I screamed, my knees buckling beneath me. Wilder held me up, his lips twisting in a triumphant grin.

"The rift must not open," he whispered into my ear. "Arondight must remain lost. *She wants him to see.*"

I coughed, the taste of blood thick on my tongue. I didn't understand.

I gasped, choking. I didn't understand because this wasn't Wilder.

He wrenched the blade free and I fell to my knees, my hands clutching uselessly at my stomach. Red. There was red everywhere. Hot, sticky…*copper.*

I had to get away. I had to warn the others.

Wilder leaned against the wall, his eyes glued to mine.

"You're… you're just going to watch me die?" I asked, tears falling unchecked from my eyes.

"How else am I going to make sure you're dead?"

"Just end it," I whispered, the pain bordering on unbearable. I didn't know death could feel like this. I mean, dying wasn't something anyone did on a daily basis, but I didn't expect it to be so *exhausting.* I guess that was the massive blood loss talking.

"And deny myself the satisfaction?" He laughed and shook his head, inspecting his blood-coated arondight blade.

My head lolled and my thoughts became fuzzy. If

I used my power against him, I risked ripping open another rift, but if I didn't, I was going to die at the feet of the man I loved.

I had to let Arondight back in. I couldn't avoid who I was, though I wasn't expecting to learn the lesson quite so soon.

I smashed through the barrier I'd slammed down on the Indigo Flame and breathed deeply, blood rattling in my chest. So I was drowning now? Which would end me first? It scarcely mattered at this point. As long as I could get back to Jackson and Esme, then I could warn them about Wilder, and they could hide the Codex.

Without the Twin Flames, the rift wouldn't be able to open *or* close. Things would stay the same as long as Mordred could be defeated. The Naturals had come back from the brink before, and I knew they could do it again.

There was still a chance to save the world. It wouldn't be the ultimate save, but it would still be here. Humanity would survive. It was better than nothing, right?

Looking up at Wilder, I narrowed my eyes and tugged on my Light.

"Having second thoughts about dying, huh?" he asked, raising an eyebrow.

"Yeah, something like that."

Everyone had an aura, but Wilder…he was missing something all right. He was colourless. Nothing. He'd lost the thing that made him who he was. His soul was gone and with it, Excalibur.

I didn't know what it meant or if his soul could be retrieved, but I knew I could fight him without fear of combining the Flames with hate.

Something he'd said hadn't made much sense, though. *Arondight must remain lost.* Did he—or whatever had control over him—not know the truth about me? If that was true, then I held the element of surprise.

"I know you're not Wilder," I said, blood dripping from my lips. "Not really. I'm not going to feel guilty for kicking your arse."

"You're going to fight me with your internal organs shredded?" He snorted and pushed off the wall. Twisting his arondight blade around, he pointed it at me. "I'd like to see you try."

"There's a lot you don't know."

"They told me you disappeared." He knelt in front of me and tilted his head to the side. Dipping his finger in the blood that oozed from between my lips, he rubbed it between his forefinger and thumb and snorted. "Obviously, that was a lie."

Man, soulless Wilder was even more of an arsehole than the regular one.

"Like I said, *there's a lot you don't know.*" My hand shot up and slammed my palm on his face, pushing a burst of indigo flame into his mind.

Wilder's head snapped back and he fell to the ground, his eyes open and unseeing. I fell over him, checking his pulse, and when I found it to be strong, I scrambled to my feet.

Red and blue lights flashed in the courtyard as the emergency services began to swarm around the area.

A group of police in full ballistic getup with automatic rifles rushed past us in formation, none of them seeing through my cloak.

I couldn't do anything for Wilder, so I left him there concealed by Light. I didn't know how long he'd be unconscious, but knowing his power, it would probably be a handful of minutes.

I stumbled down the alley, my shoulder hitting the wall. Grunting in pain, I took a right and headed away from Seven Dials. When I found another alley, I ducked into the murky shadows, wanting to keep off the main road. There was no telling what else was lurking out there, waiting for me.

"*Scarlett.*"

Wilder's voice echoed down they alley, mocking like a serial killer stalking his prey. I stumbled against the wall, leaving a smear of blood behind like a trail of breadcrumbs.

"*Scarlett…* you can't run from me."

This wasn't right. I was Arondight. I could heal other people and bring them back from the brink of death and that was before I'd been awakened. I had my full power now, so why couldn't I heal myself?

I stumbled and fell, landing awkwardly on my arm. Pain exploded thought my body and as I dragged myself behind a dumpster, I wondered why I wasn't dead yet. Any normal person would've bled out by now.

The stench of rotting rubbish hovered around me as I curled into a ball. I was on fire, it seared through my veins and clouded my mind.

No one was coming to help me. No one at all.

I slid my hands under my T-shirt and hissed as I disturbed my torn flesh. Man, it felt as if I had one serious case of stomach acid.

"Arondight," I murmured, tears streaming down my face, "*help… me.*"

My lips numbed and I fell against the side of the dumpster. I heaved, throwing up blood and bile onto the ground, my forehead prickling with sweat.

Man, dying sucked balls. Not just any balls—gigantic, sweaty hairy ones.

My eyes drooped and I called out to anyone who'd listen, but the words never reached my lips—Jackson, Wilder, Aldrich, Aiden, *Galahad*.

Mother. Father.

A snort echoed above.

"In the trash, where you're supposed to be," Wilder mused, looking down at me. "Honestly, I'm impressed you made it this far. I thought you would've dropped dead by now."

"You're… not… him…" I rasped, shaking. Warmth sparked inside me, taking me by surprise. Imagining the flame burning through the corruption inside my body, I guided and shaped the Light. *It was working.*

"I am," he said, unaware of what was happening inside me. "All those years, I was shunned by my own people." He shook his head and kneeled beside me. "Hated, feared, pushed aside." He ran his fingers through my hair. "To think I wanted to be one of them is *laughable* now that I know true freedom."

"Your soul—"

"*Was a curse.*"

"No," I whispered, tensing as the ragged flesh of my stomach knitted back together. "Your salvation was stolen from you, and I'm going to get it back." I raised my hand and wrapped my fingers around his wrist. "I'm going to save you, Wilder. You'll see."

I pushed a burst of Light at him and his eyes widened a split-second before he was thrown clear across the alley. He collided against the wall, the bang echoing off the surrounding buildings.

I scrambled to my feet and grasped for the arondight blade I'd taken from the cache at the safe house, then tore the cold iron dagger out of my boot. Standing, I brought the arondight blade to life, wielding it in my right hand and brandishing the dagger in my left.

Wilder recovered quickly, just as I knew he would.

He glared at me with pure anger, his arondight blade sparking silver. He didn't have his Flame, but it didn't matter, a Natural's power was in their body, not their soul—it was how I could still use my Light when I blocked out Arondight.

"You can heal yourself now?"

"I can do a lot of things," I told him.

"It's better if you die, Scarlett. We are fighting a war that can never be won." He lunged, his sword slicing through the air and I ducked, kicking out with my right leg.

My heel slammed into his knee and it buckled underneath him, but he used the momentum of his swing to spin in a complete circle and rise, striking as I stood.

The blade hissed through the air, narrowly missing my side and I dropped my arondight blade. With my left hand, I slammed the cold iron dagger into his shoulder.

Wilder roared in pain and I smashed my right elbow against the side of his head. His grip loosened on his sword and he faltered, giving me just enough time to hit him again, this time with a little help from Arondight.

He slumped to the ground and I fell onto my arse, my chest heaving.

Wilder had attacked me with the intent to kill. Wilder, the man I was in love with. Of course, it wasn't him, and I had no idea what to do now that he was lying on the ground out cold with a dagger sticking out of his shoulder. There was nowhere to hold him in the safe house, and who knew where the hell his soul was.

I had to leave him.

Grabbing both our arondight blades, I let them retract into their hilts and shoved them into my jacket pocket.

Kneeling over Wilder, I smoothed back his hair and kissed his forehead. His skin was clammy, yet cool to the touch. I blinked as a flake of snow fell gently over us and landed in his hair. Looking towards the sky, I held back a wave of despair as the first drops of winter fluttered silently from the heavens.

I swallowed the tightness in my throat as I gazed at Wilder.

"I'll come back for you," I murmured. "I'll find your soul and give it back…and together, we'll punish the monsters who took it. *I promise.*" Touching his shoulder, I placed a veil of protection over him. "There's so much I need to tell you. *So much.*"

I rose to my feet and with one last look, I disappeared into the city.

8

———————

I stumbled up the front stairs of the safe house and collapsed against the door.

I'd like to say I had the strength to hold myself together, but as I'd made my way across the city, with sirens blaring in the distance, I came apart one stitch at time.

The Twin Flames must come together in love… I'd seen what power I could wrought when hate filled my heart, but how could I find love within myself when so many that I cared about had died? How could I risk the world like that?

No one will ever love a freak like you.

What a time to think about Sally Mathewson, the bully who'd made my life a living hell in high school —at least the last one I'd gone to. That's where this began though, right? The deep-rooted psychological issues that screwed up adulthood could always be traced back to the one moment where you were at your lowest in your formative years. I didn't know if the day Sally Mathewson said those words to me was my 'moment', but it was close enough.

I clutched my stomach, the sensation of Wilder's blade ripping through my innards still fresh in my mind. My T-shirt was stiff with dried blood and my fingers were tacky with it.

The door opened behind me and I fell backwards, my head hitting the uneven floor.

"Scarlett!" Esme exclaimed. "You're covered in blood—"

"Get her inside. Quick." *Jackson*.

"I should've let it go," I whispered as they hauled me inside the house. "I should've…"

I was lying on the bed in the downstairs bedroom, lost in an ever-increasing mire of self-loathing. The ceiling paint was peeling, not that had anything to do with anything—Wilder was a terrible homeowner.

"Where did all this blood come from?" Jackson asked. "I don't see any wounds…"

"Her T-shirt is torn, but—"

"It's mine," I rasped, my head beginning to clear. Whatever my body was doing to heal itself was finally working its way away from my stomach.

"Yours?" Jackson smoothed my hair away from my face. "How?"

"How do I do anything?" I replied wryly. "How do I heal a demon-hybrid with acidic blood? How do I heal a knight impaled on a demon's claw? How do I kill a greater demon?" I coughed, grimacing as a sharp stabbing pain tore through my stomach. "I make it up as I go along."

"You healed yourself?" Esme asked.

"*Surprise.*"

Jackson tugged on my hand. "What happened?"

"I—"

What should I tell them? How could I explain the fact that I'd literally ripped apart half the city with the mystical power wrapped around my soul? The more I thought about it, the crazier it sounded. I was a risk to everyone and everything. The war had spilled over into the human world and it was all my fault. I had too much hate in my heart.

The night Markzoth had murdered my parents was the moment the Dark had won. I just didn't understand it until now. As long as there was hate in me, we'd never be at peace.

No one will ever love a freak like you.

That feeling of foreboding I'd had at Brax's funeral was right on the money. Arondight should've remained lost.

"I found him," I murmured, my stomach aching. "He—"

"*Wilder?*"

I nodded. "He's missing his soul, that's why I can't find him."

"He's lost his soul?" Esme glanced at Jackson, her expression troubled.

"Something took it and now… Now he doesn't want to come back." I sat up and swatted them away. "The things he said—" He'd said his soul was a curse. *A curse.* Maybe it was—having Arondight awoken in me hadn't been the blessing I'd hoped for.

But the Wilder I knew wouldn't willingly give up that part of himself. He'd made peace with who he believed he was meant to be, despite his differences. Someone had taken him by force and prized his soul from him against his will.

"Scarlett…" Jackson knelt beside the bed, "did he do this to you?"

"He's not himself."

Jackson cursed and lowered his gaze.

"I've done worse," I hissed. "Wilder attacked me and we fought, but *I've done worse.*"

"You've done nothing wrong, Scarlett," he argued. "You've—"

"I blew up a busy footpath in Covent Garden last night. Then I blew up the courtyard at Seven Dials. All because I had hate in my heart when I called Arondight for help. Wilder doesn't have his soul but I do, and I'm beginning to think it's hopeless."

Jackson and Esme glanced at one another, both remaining tight-lipped. They didn't know what to do about it, either. It wasn't like we could Google the troubleshooting guide for celestial beings. There wasn't a Reddit sub-forum for that.

"You're like Dark Phoenix," Jackson said after a moment.

I scowled. "Who's Dark Phoenix?"

"From *X-Men*," he explained. "Her mutant abilities were tied to an otherworldly creature known as the Phoenix, an uncontrollable entity with terrible power."

I didn't like the sound of it, and it was a fictional

story, but it felt too similar to discount, especially when I was grasping for answers which weren't coming. "What happened to her?"

"Well, it depends on which version of the story you read…" He coughed nervously. "She tried to destroy the world and the only way she could be stopped was when Wolverine used his mutant healing ability to fight her power and, uh…kill her."

"Why would you say that to her?" Esme cried, slapping him on the arm.

"It's just a story," I murmured, hugging my arms around my middle.

An awkward silence fell over the three of us.

Jackson coughed. "Where's Wilder now?"

"I don't know." He would've woken up by now. Who knows where he would've scurried away to? "I didn't have the strength to bring him back. We've nowhere to put him anyway."

"We have to find him and get his soul back," Jackson said. "He has the right to know the truth about who he is."

"He seemed so sincere," I whispered, tears welling in my eyes. "It might've been taken from him by force, but—"

"No." Jackson grasped my shoulders and forced me to look at him. "You and I both know what kind of man Wilder is. He'd never give up who he is. He'd fight until he dropped."

"You didn't see how he was when you were gone," Esme murmured. "He turned over Heaven and Earth looking for you."

And I owed him the same.

I wouldn't be whole until I brought him back, and Arondight would continue to be unpredictable until its Twin Flame burned beside it. I knew what I had to do, but what if I couldn't trust myself? Collateral damage was unacceptable. If I continued this way, I risked plunging the entire world into Darkness.

"What if I hurt someone tonight?" I whispered, barely holding onto my tears. "What if I killed an innocent?" Jackson and Esme looked at one another with troubled expressions. "Then all of this will be for nothing. I'll tear apart the rift and it'll all be over. Everything—" I choked back a sob and wiped my damp eyes.

"You don't know that," Jackson argued. "We can't say what'll happen, Scarlett. The future is unwritten, remember?"

He spoke Gilhana's prophecy with such conviction, that I threw my arms around his neck and sobbed into his shirt.

Esme laid her hand on my shoulder. "One step at a time," she reassured me quietly. "First, we get you cleaned up and rested, then we find Wilder. We'll worry about the rest later."

I let Jackson go and wiped my tears. She was right —there was nothing else I could do right now, not in my state. I had to pull myself together and carry out the promise I'd made to Wilder.

I'd find his soul, return it to him, punish those who harmed him, and then he could make up his mind if he wanted to be awoken as Excalibur.

He deserved that at least.

<hr>

I knew I'd been dreaming when I woke up.

It was one of those surreal images that faded the moment consciousness began to creep in, erasing the memory immediately. Whatever it had been, it mustn't have been important.

Rolling over, I saw a set of clean clothes had been left on the floor beside the bed, folded into a neat pile. Someone had scrubbed my boots, wiped down my leather jacket, and had washed and dried my trousers and underwear. *Esme.*

It was a shame she and Jackson had met under such trying circumstances, but I'd stopped questioning fate around the time I fell into a lake during the Middle Ages.

I dragged myself out of bed and inspected my stomach. No mark remained to betray what had went down, and I was glad I didn't have a constant reminder of Wilder's soulless attempt at murdering me. It wasn't him, but his face…

I shook my head, dislodging the unwelcome thought, and dressed. My limbs were stiff from last night's misadventures, my eyes gritty with sleep.

When I finally emerged from the bedroom, the front door opened and closed as I stepped into the hall. I turned, my heart thrumming.

Esme's gaze met mine and she flushed as Jackson ran down the stairs, his hair sticking up in all directions like he'd rammed his finger into a power point. He was in various states of undress, which meant he'd either been caught sleeping or he was in a mad rush to get dressed so he could find his missing girlfriend. I voted for the latter.

"Where have you been?" he cried. *Bingo.*

She rolled her eyes and closed the door behind her. "Calm down."

"Calm down?" He flailed his arms and I leaned against the doorjamb. "The entire world is crawling with demons and you went out to the shops?"

"I went to the *Off-Licence* down the hill," she replied with a pout. "They had some cheap pay-as-you-go phones."

"You went out for a phone?"

"We need information, Jackson." She tossed her hair over her shoulder and strode down the hall past me.

I looked up at Jackson and shrugged. "Nice hairdo."

He dragged his fingers through his unruly mop and made a face. "It's not safe out there."

"It's marginally safer for a demon-hybrid than a Natural right now." I smiled and followed Esme into the kitchen.

She had opened the box and was putting the phone together as I sat down. "It's not the latest iPhone, but it'll get us what we need to know."

"Don't you need ID to get one of those?" Jackson asked, emerging from behind me. "How—"

"Don't fuss, Jackson," she scolded. "I watch all the crime shows. I know how to get a burner phone."

"Modern women," I stated, thinking about the Naturals at Castle Brent and the humans at Castle Bourke. Ladies and warriors.

"Yeah," Esme declared with a pout, "don't underestimate girl power." She jammed the charger into the wall and flicked on the switch.

I stared as she began to fiddle with the phone, seeing an image of Wilder doing the same as we sat in a coffee shop in Waterloo Station. It felt like eons ago that we'd been on the run, searching for the Necropolis. We were on our own now, and I hadn't realised just how much he'd done for me until I had to do it myself.

"The explosion at Seven Dials was ruled a gas leak according to the Daily Mail," Esme exclaimed, breaking me out of my haze. "No one was hurt."

My heart skipped a hopeful beat as I realised what she'd risked herself for—my peace of mind. "The market?"

"Hang on…" She swiped her thumb across the screen, looking for an article. "The explosion at Covent Garden… The source is unknown and investigations continue. There were several people with minor injuries, but no one was seriously hurt."

I sighed in relief and pressed my forehead against the table. The lacquered wood was cool on my fevered brow and I squeezed my eyes shut, trying to hold in a flood of relieved tears.

"Everyone's in a fuss about it though, but that's

not a surprise," she added. "Now we have to figure out how to track down Wilder."

"Scarlett, you said something about the city lighting up," Jackson said, "that night we were sitting on the roof of the Sanctum."

I raised my head and nodded. "I can see people's auras. It's like a rainbow." A rainbow that reminded me of the Druids and their meddlesome prisms.

"Are auras linked to souls?" Esme asked.

I shrugged. "I don't know. Maybe? I'm trying to figure it out as I go. I never knew much about all that spiritual hippy stuff."

"Hippy stuff?" Esme laughed. "Well, if they are, it stands to reason you can sense souls, too." She looked to Jackson with hope. "Wilder's soul is linked with Excalibur, like yours is with Arondight, so you know what it looks like."

"The Twin Flames call out to each other," I murmured.

"Exactly! Wherever his soul is, it's calling out to yours. You can use that."

Brax. The memory of him slammed into my mind with unbelievable force. "What if his soul is gone? Like Brax's."

Jackson's lips thinned. He'd thought about it too, but he'd already came up with a conclusion. "I highly doubt a soul like yours or Wilder's is as destructible as a human or Natural's. Power like that is a prize. Whoever has it, would likely use it as leverage."

Leverage… I turned the word over in my mind, puzzling it out. It stood to reason that the Dark had their own internal politics just like we did. They were not one entity.

"If I focus on the Earth, maybe I can pick out the anomalies from all the noise." I rubbed my temples. "But there's so many people here, I don't know if I can filter out all the nonsense."

"Sounds like the Wild West of the Internet," Jackson drawled. "You need a browser extension to block all the pop-ups."

"Some still get through. At least on my laptop."

"Don't be so defeatist."

"You can try some meditation techniques," Esme suggested. "It's all about calming the mind and filtering out the noise. Or you could give astral projection a go." She may as well have been speaking an alien language to me.

"I'm going up to the roof so I can contemplate the glory of the universe," I said dryly.

"That's what I usually do on the toilet," Jackson said, attempting a joke.

My lips quirked and I shot Esme a sympathetic look. "I'm going up on the roof to give this thing a try."

"You want some company?"

I shook my head as I stood. "No, it's okay. I think this is something I have to do on my own."

Leaving the kitchen, I grabbed my jacket and went upstairs. I climbed out onto the roof via the front bedroom window and ducked under the eave. It was cold as the Arctic out here, and I flipped up the collar of my jacket to shield the back of my neck against the chill.

Sitting on the tiles, I kicked my feet across the gutter and over the edge of the roof. Swinging my boots back and forth, I looked over the lights which lit the hillside and suburbs beyond.

Somewhere out there a battle was raging. Naturals were fighting the Dark that was sweeping through the streets. Mordred was lingering some place, concocting a scheme to track me and the Codex down. Aldrich, Greer, and the others were amassing in an attempt to save as much of our legacy as possible before we could hope to strike back. And there were so many more missing souls who may or may not be dead, infected, or worse.

Wilder…

I let my mind soar as I'd done the night I'd been out with Hunter on the banks of the Thames—the same night I'd found the alpha site. As I took in the city below, I wondered if this was what Esme meant by astral projection.

No matter what it was called, I hoped I was doing it right. The Lady of the Lake seemed to think I'd know what to do when the time came. I always thought she meant when Wilder and I finally stood before the rift, but maybe it was more than that. Maybe I had to stop being so logical about things and just trust that Arondight would guide me.

Hey, Purples.

It was Wilder. He was calling out to me!

My eyes flew open and I almost expected to see

him sitting beside me, but I was alone on the roof. I breathed deeply, my breath vaporising in plumes in front of me.

Wilder?

There was no response, but I wasn't sure I was totally expecting one, either. His presence felt like an echo, or maybe it was his unconscious sensing I was near and was calling out to me.

I focused and attempted to grasp the thread of familiarity that was Wilder's voice. The city ebbed and flowed below and suddenly, I stopped.

A ball of strangeness lingered amongst the aura of London's inhabitants. It was a storm of white noise that hissed so loud it reminded me of a raging waterfall. It was lodged in an area of muddy brown and grey like a wadded-up ball of paper tumbling around in a clothes dryer. I'd never seen anything like it, but then again, I was in uncharted territory.

Hey, Purples. His voice came to me again and I knew it was a layer of residual energy that only he could've left behind.

I opened my eyes and yelped as I realised Jackson was sitting beside me. "Holy crap on a stick!" I exclaimed.

"Sorry," he said with a smirk. "You've been out here for ages. I just wanted to make sure you didn't fall off."

I shook my head. I'd only been out of my head for a few minutes, hadn't I?

"I think I've found him," I said. "I have to go and see to make sure, though."

"You're going out there alone? *Again*?" He sighed. "*Scarlett…*"

I lowered my gaze. "So much of this I'm going to have to do on my own, Jackson."

"You are allowed to ask for help."

"I know. It's just…" I trailed off, not knowing how to explain it. What I was going through seemed to be an incredibly personal thing. Then there were the confusing and overwhelming things I felt for Wilder. The last time I saw him, he told me he didn't know what was in his heart and hearing it hadn't been easy.

Jackson knocked his shoulder against mine. "What is it?"

"What if he doesn't love me?" I blurted.

"*Pfft*. He'd be stupid not to. Aren't you fated or something? Twin Flames?"

"I'm not sure it works that way."

"The Lady of the Lake said you had to use love to repair what was broken, right?"

I nodded.

"But there are all kinds of love."

I knew he was only trying to comfort me and provide a little hope, but romantic love…well, it was gut-wrenching.

I grunted and shoved away my fickle human heart. It didn't matter what I felt right now. Wilder was out there without his soul. No one deserved that fate. No one at all.

"I'll be back soon," I told Jackson. "Don't wait up."

And with that, I jumped off the edge of the roof, landed on the footpath below, and disappeared into the city.

9

Mayfair was probably one of the poshest places in London outside of royal residences.

Arondight had led me through the city, the minuscule trace Wilder had left behind guiding me to this spot. *Here*, my mind told me. *He is here.*

I looked up at the mansion with its stone façade and dark widows with narrowed eyes. I could feel the same concentration of strangeness that I'd sensed from the safe house. It was ebbing from underneath the front door like a primordial ooze straight out of a *Goosebumps* novel.

I walked up the stairs and twisted the doorknob. This was one time I was within my rights not to knock. Somehow, I figured the butler had been laid off centuries ago.

The door creaked inwards, squeaking and groaning as it revealed a dark entryway beyond. This was so the same thing as when people ran up the stairs in horror movies. I was stepping into the danger zone, knowing full well that I could be fighting pure Darkness the moment the door closed behind me.

Still, I went inside. Getting Wilder back was worth facing the proverbial Freddy Kruger of the demon world.

The house was dark, but I had no trouble making out the level of fancy through the gloom. It looked like it hadn't changed since the day it was built, apart from the layer of dust. I had no idea about architecture or furniture styles, but it looked like something out of a BBC period drama—a Jane Austen retelling in mini-series form—with all the trimmings. Maybe it was sixteenth century? It was hard to say.

The walls were wallpapered with a fleur-de-lis motif, the French stylised fern repeating over and over, the pattern only breaking where paintings with golden filigree frames hung—portraits of men in English redcoats and ladies in frilly dresses. Empty eyes followed me down the hall, making the hairs on the back of my neck stand up.

Dust was all over the floor and had piled up in the corners like sand dunes. My boots left prints behind me and I shivered, wondering if there wasn't something more sinister. Were there other kinds of demons out there? Ones we didn't know about? Possession was one thing, but demons who could take souls was a terrifying thought.

My hands shook as I approached the first door

leading off the hall. I wasn't welcome here. I felt the cold hostility all around me, and when I breathed in, the ashes of it settled in my lungs.

When my eyes had fully adjusted to the murky light, I realised each door I passed had a dull silvery glow around the edges, giving the hallway a creepy haunted feeling. Something shone just beyond, luring me deeper into the house.

What the hell…?

Pressing my palm against the door, I hissed and jerked away as noise filled my mind. Voices. Screams, wails, crying, sobbing.

Get a grip, Scarlett, I thought. *Wilder's soul could be in here somewhere.*

Taking a deep breath, I turned the handle and eased the door open. Peering through the crack, I gasped as I saw every available surface stacked high with glass jars of all shapes and sizes, each of them filled with glowing silver orbs.

I closed the door and went to the next room and found more. It was a grand ballroom, the ornate ceiling crowned with a crystal chandelier which reflected the pale bluish glow. It reminded me of ice, as if I was standing in a palace of the stuff, but in this story, the icicles were glowing balls of light.

There were rows upon rows of them, stacked up to the ceiling like cans in a supermarket. I'd never seen such a thing in my life.

This time, I stepped inside and picked up a jar from where it was perched on top of a stack on a side table. The orb tapped against the side as I tilted the canister and I held it up so I could study it.

"Oh my god."

It was a soul. A human soul. They all were…

I looked around the room in horror at all the jars, my heart thrumming a wild tempo. There had to be thousands of them and there were another three stories above me and what felt like a level below. Were they all crammed like this one? I wasn't brave enough to find out.

Retreating back into the hall, I looked up the staircase at a skylight far above. The orange artificial glow of the city lingered beyond. If I was going to keep someone or something important locked up, I'd keep it in a dungeon.

I turned my attention downwards and I felt something tug around the edges of my Light. I sucked in a deep breath and descended into the bowels of the house.

It was a large dungeon-like basement—the walls were stacked with uneven clumps of bluestone with a modern concrete floor. It stunk like dampness and mould, the air chilling through the exposed skin of my face and hands.

The shadows were absolute the farther I moved away from the staircase. Holding up my hand, I called on my Light and summoned a tiny ball of glowing purple flame to illuminate my way.

I gasped as the eerie light revealed a body lying on a table in front of me. As I stepped closer, my heart jerked when I realised who it was.

Wilder.

I rushed forwards and gritted my teeth. Leather belts with metal ties were wrapped around each wrist and around his middle. I fumbled with the buckles, my touch rousing him. His head shot up and I let out a startled yelp.

"Who are you?" he demanded, the violet light casting a menacing glow across his features.

"Wilder, it's me…Scarlett. I've come to get you. I—"

"Who are you?" he roared as if he hadn't heard me. "I will get out of here and when I do, I will *tear you apart*."

I stared at him in shock. He didn't recognise me. Without his soul, he was lost and his memories were dust. He was a shell of his former self. I didn't know what drove him or what remained of his consciousness, but the man who lay before me wasn't Wilder. Not really.

"I wouldn't do that if I were you."

I paused at the hostile voice and the presence of Darkness flowed into the room.

Turning, I bristled as a tall, striking woman sashayed into the room. She looked like a six-foot-tall catwalk model with the perfect lean body and flawless ivory skin. Tight chestnut ringlets framed her pouty lips, and bright green eyes zeroed in on me with laser precision. High heels and a slinky dress were involved, but I was too busy internally retching at her blatant demonic essence to take much notice.

Glamazon. That was the first word that popped into my mind and my hackles rose. Of all the stupid things in the world to think, I had to get jealous of a good-looking demon who had obviously taken too much liberty with glamour illusions. Strike a pose, indeed.

She was a demon, there was no doubt about it, but her Darkness was like nothing I'd ever felt before. It was cold as the Arctic and when she looked upon me, I had the sensation of an otherworldly emptiness —a maw so dark and deep, nothing could fill it.

I supposed that's why her creepy arse hoarded jars of souls looked like she had forgotten her feather duster.

"Who are you?" I demanded. "What have you done to him?"

"He's so pretty, don't you agree?" Her voice was like a siren call and it sent a shiver through me. Was that how she did it? How she lured unsuspecting people into her trap so she could suck the very humanity out of their bodies? What a creep.

"Answer the question."

"The question?" the woman asked, tilting her head to the side. "But you asked two." She stepped closer, her cool gaze raking over me. "Your soul is… mmm, exquisite." She reached out for me and I slapped her hand away, indigo flame zapping. "Interesting. Interesting, indeed."

"I'll ask you one last time…" I seethed. "Who. Are. You?"

"I am the Grey Lady."

I snorted. "Think highly of ourselves, do we?"

The woman snarled, her form phasing into a grotesque glowing corpse and back again so fast that I didn't have time to cry out in fright. I wasn't fond of jump scares, and I scowled at her.

"I can see why you don't go for the natural look," I drawled. The Grey Lady, indeed. It wasn't her true name, but I knew those held power over her kind and there was no way she was giving her true identity to the likes of me.

"Insolence. I could prize your soul from your body and turn you into a withered husk," she threatened.

I narrowed my eyes. "You and I both know you can't take anything from me."

The Grey Lady's lips curved into a twisted smile and her gaze flickered down as if she was seeing into my spiritual essence, then rose to meet my eyes.

"No," she said. "I cannot hope to possess Arondight."

"Then we can skip the pomp and get straight to the point. Give me back the Natural and his soul, and we won't have any trouble here."

"I think we can come to an arrangement, though I'm not sure it will be to your liking."

It rarely was, but I allowed my Light to flare. The Grey Lady scoffed and flicked her hair in a very pouty human-like way.

"There will be no arrangement. You know what I can do to you and I won't hesitate."

"We shall see." She smirked and I knew a twist

was coming. A double-cross was the most likely item on the menu, but not knowing exactly what she was threw a big fat unknown into the mix. I'd have to play this one by ear and hope I was smart enough.

She undid his restraints, her heels clicking against the concrete as she moved around the table, making a show of her supposed benevolence. Finally, she leaned over Wilder, draping herself over his body. "Come, my pet," she purred, running a fingertip seductively down his cheek. She looked at me, her lips curving into a sly grin. "You must be precious if the Celestial has come for you."

Celestial? I scowled at her and nodded towards the stairs. "Take me to his soul."

She huffed and sashayed across the basement, Wilder following her like a lost puppy.

I scowled, my grip tightening on my arondight blade. I hated seeing him like that—Wilder, the strong, stubborn warrior who I'd fallen in love with. If I wanted his soul, then there was nothing to do but find out where they were going.

The Grey Lady led me back to the ballroom. As we stood just outside, the souls began to tap against their jars and the sound would've been magical if it wasn't at the expense of thousands of innocents, but instead, it only made my heart twist even more. I had to be careful here—I didn't want a repeat of Seven Dials.

I looked at Wilder, but his eyes were downcast and his expression was empty.

"If you want to free him, you must choose," the Grey Lady said, pushing me into the room. "You have one chance, so pick wisely."

The door slammed closed behind me and I whirled, dropping my swords and banging my fists against the wood. When it didn't budge, I rattled the door handle, but I was locked inside by more than a deadlock. I was positive I could totally blow the thing off its hinges with a flick of my wrist, but it wouldn't do me any good. The Grey Lady had tricked me into the ultimate *Where's Wally* challenge.

Turned out I wasn't as smart as I thought I was.

Turning, I took a deep breath and stared at the mountains of jars before me. Excalibur and Arondight called out for one another, so this should be easy, right? I looked around at the never-ending corridor of souls and grimaced. *Wrong.*

The parallels with the Holy Grail story from the Arthurian legends were almost ironic—as was the *Indiana Jones and the Last Crusade* reference. A room full of cups, all of them different and only one was the prize I sought. Choosing incorrectly would see my death.

My gaze ran over jar after jar, the contents looking the same as the one before it. None of these were Wilder. Each one represented a life, but not the one I sought.

Even if I managed to free him, what about all these imprisoned souls? They'd remain here forever, lost and unable to move on. I couldn't just leave them here. If the Grey Lady wouldn't free them, then I would.

I raised my hand and called for my Light.

The door slammed open and the Lady rushed in, her true form showing through the glamour she'd woven around her grotesque body. Darkness whipped at my arms, forcing my Light to darkness.

"Your test is a farce," I hissed. "I won't be a part of your games."

Wilder stood behind her, his gaze moving between us. Where he was blank before, now there was an echo of what had driven him to confront me at Seven Dials. Was it him, or the Lady?

"What do you want from me?" he snarled.

The Lady let me go and turned to her prize. If I killed her, what would happen to the souls she'd collected?

"You belong to me," she told him. "That's what I want." She laughed then, running her fingertips along his face. "Such a handsome Natural you are. It was so easy to lure you here. She can't see past it, but I can." The sound of her laughter filled the ballroom with echoes of splintering crystal.

"I can see past what he is," I snarled. "I want him for *who* he is."

"What I am?" Wilder whispered, staring at the floor.

The Lady turned and looked at him curiously. "You couldn't feel it inside you? Surely it must've burned a hole into your very being." She caressed his face with her icy hands and placed her ear to his chest like she was listening for something. "His echo speaks to me! Can you not hear it?"

This bitch was crazy. I grasped the hilt of my arondight blade and tore it free. Violet sparks skittered across the floor as the sword clicked together.

"It doesn't matter which jar holds his soul," I declared. "When I set them all free, they'll return to where they belong."

"No!" she shrieked, lunging for me.

I let loose, indigo flame exploding outwards and the jars shattered. The crack was deafening, then the shards began to fall like torrential rain, tinkling as they hit the floor of the ballroom. Sharp points bounced off me, leaving no mark and the Lady fell to her knees, sobbing like a spoilt princess.

For a moment, nothing seemed to happen, but then all at once the room filled with a storm of glowing orbs that rushed towards the open door like a fevered tornado of swarming bees. They tore at my hair and clothes as they passed, the identities of each one grazing against my own. My mind was stuffed full of memories that didn't belong to me, and then they disappeared just as suddenly.

I reached out as I sensed a familiar whirl in the storm, but before I could grasp it, it rushed past and slammed into Wilder's chest, throwing him against the wall like a rag doll.

"What have you done?" the Grey Lady shrieked, her voice distorting as her glamour began to fail.

Before I could answer, Wilder let out a wail of pain so harsh it nearly brought me to my knees.

He rose, tears of pure silver dripping from his eyes, and approached the Grey Lady. Each step stoked the flame growing inside him and Arondight flared in response, pulling me towards him.

Excalibur was awakening.

Wilder continued to burn as he lifted himself from the floor, liquid fire sizzling where it hit the shards of glass. It took every ounce of his strength to lift himself towards the demon directly before him. I could feel the rage inside him, the anger at what the Lady had done to him.

The fire built within him made his eyes glow with silver flame. Abruptly, he cried out in pain, a terrible wail which tore through my soul and stirred Arondight. Falling towards the demon, he grabbed her neck with both hands. She screamed in pain as her flesh melted from her bones, the room filling with the putrid stench of burning flesh.

I looked on in horror, not knowing what to do. If I helped him, I risked Arondight joining with Excalibur before we were ready. Wilder was full of rage for the creature who'd imprisoned him—his awakening terrible and uncontrollable. Knowing what I'd already done on my own, I couldn't risk tearing open the way between worlds.

There was nothing I could do but wait until it was over.

Wilder screamed at the demon, pooling all his physical pain and mental anguish into his cry. The

Argent Flame poured from within him so bright that it stunned me to silence as the Grey Lady disintegrated under his touch. Her body glowed like hot coals before it crumbled to ash in his hands.

Wilder fell to the floor, his body steaming and hissing against the moisture in the air. I rushed forwards, ignoring the demon-shaped pile of ash on the floor, and grasped his face as he curled himself into a ball. He whimpered, his shoulders shuddering.

I touched his fevered cheek with my cool hand and he flinched violently. I jerked away from his reaction, but when I saw the recognition in his eyes, I crawled back, placing my hand against his forehead.

"It's okay," I murmured. "I've got you."

"Purples?" he whispered.

"Yes." I stroked his damp hair away from his brow and eased his head into my lap. "It's my turn to save you, you know. No more cotton wool."

He coughed and I felt the flame subside inside him. Arondight simmered happily and it was the strangest sensation. I tingled all over as I held Wilder in my arms, the surrounding destruction forgotten.

He gripped my forearm and his worried gaze met mine. "What's happening to me?"

"You're awakening…" I told him. "As your true self."

"My true self?" he sobbed, lost in the confusion of his ordeal.

"I'll explain everything, I promise."

"Where were you, Purples?" he croaked.

"It's a long story." I sighed and held him close, the

intimacy of our embrace not lost on me. "C'mon, let's get you out of here."

As I helped Wilder to his feet, and we left the house of horrors behind us, I knew I'd never look at a mason jar the same way again.

10

———

The sun rose over London and the city woke up, humans going about their usual business. Trains rolled over rails, pulling in and out of stations. Busses took to the streets, loading up on passengers on their way to work. The consumer machine was gearing up for another day of trading as I watched over Wilder's sleeping form.

I sat on the end of the bed, my back resting against the wall and watched him sleep. It was kind of creepy but being apart for so long, I didn't want to let him out of my sight.

Blinking, I couldn't shake the image of liquid fire dripping from his eyes. He seemed okay physically—although exhausted—but mentally…? When he woke, I'd have to drop the motherload onto him.

The bedroom door eased open and I glanced up at Jackson. He held out a bowl of steaming porridge. "Hungry?"

"Thanks." I took the bowl from him and held it

against my chest, warming myself. Grasping the spoon, I began to shovel porridge into my mouth.

"Are you cold?" he asked. "The boiler seems to be on the fritz, but I'll have a look at it."

"Since when are you a handyman?"

"Since my girlfriend snuck out of the house and risked her life to get a mobile phone, I can Google it."

I smirked at him and raised my eyebrows. That was the first time he'd referred to Esme as his girlfriend. Honestly, I wondered what had taken him so long.

"What's that look for?" he asked with a frown.

"You called Esme your girlfriend."

His cheeks flushed a pretty shade of red and I cupped my hands around the bowl of porridge.

"I'm happy for you," I went on. "God knows we need a little of it right now."

"Esme's been looking for the others," he told me, nodding towards the kitchen. "Do you wanna talk?"

I glanced at Wilder, but he hadn't budged. Nodding, I left him to rest and went with Jackson into the kitchen. I set my bowl on the table then slipped into a chair at the end.

"He still hasn't woken up?" Esme asked, glancing up from the mobile phone.

I shook my head. "Not even to turn over."

"When you healed me, you were out like that," Jackson said. "You didn't move an inch until you suddenly woke up."

I nodded. "He'll wake when he's ready."

"What happened out there? I know you said he fought that crazy demon, but…"

"Excalibur awoke," I told them. "It was nothing like what the Lady of the Lake did to bring forth Arondight. Wilder…well, his awakening was traumatic at best." I then explained what had happened the moment his soul had returned to his body and the power he'd lost control of in the aftermath.

"Liquid fire…" Esme whispered. "Incredible."

"I doubt Wilder would say the same."

"I wonder why it was easier for you," Jackson mused.

I shrugged. "The more I think about it, the more I wonder if the night Markzoth murdered my parents was when I'd awoken. I was too young to manifest so—"

"So only a small piece of your true self was activated," Esme finished for me.

I sighed and turned my attention to the kitchen window. Outside, it'd been snowing and a thin layer of white had built up around the sill.

"How am I going to tell him?" I murmured.

"As clearly and succinctly as possible," Esme replied.

"How did you take it?" Jackson wondered. "You know, when the Lady of the Lake told you?"

I sat in silence for a moment, remembering when she told me. "Surprisingly well," I drawled. "By that point I'd traveled through time and been pursued by seven-foot-tall demons who looked like Venom—"

"Her first comic book reference," Jackson said with a sniff. "I'm so proud."

"And I'd seen a Druid turn into an eagle, and I'd travelled through a portal to a pocket of space and time separate from our world," I added in one long breath. "Being told I was Arondight didn't seem much of a stretch after all that."

"But it's not easy to convince someone else."

"You know how many times I had to explain myself to that pointless committee." I shook my head. "It's just... Everything that's happened since." Mordred, the Sanctums falling, the losses we'd suffered... How was I going to tell him when I knew he'd blame himself for not being there?

"Wilder's seen the things you can do," Jackson reassured me. "He cares about you."

"It's not about me," I murmured, stirring the spoon around the cooling bowl of porridge. "Not today."

<hr>

When I returned to the bedroom, I curled up next to Wilder. I hoped he didn't mind. He'd been a real arse the last time we shared a mattress. I smiled and nestled against the spare pillow.

What I wouldn't do to hear another self-righteous smart-arse observation from him right about now. He was always right, but couldn't resist rubbing it in.

"Purples?"

I sat up with a gasp, rubbing the grit out of my eyes. "You're awake."

"Am I?" he rasped. "I feel like shite."

"I'm so sorry," I choked out. "I said some awful things to you and just vanished. I—" I clamped my mouth shut. Our reunion was already going off the rails.

"You did, but that's not out of character, is it?"

"Wilder, I—"

"Where were you?" He breathed deeply, his fingers brushing against my thigh. "Aiden said you'd gone to find Arondight at the stones, but you weren't there… I searched for you, Scarlett, for *months*."

"1196," I said sheepishly.

His brow creased. "I don't get it."

I told him all of it. What'd happened when I found the stones. How the demons had devolved from their true forms. I told him about Galahad and our adventures across the countryside—through the Cotswolds, Castle Bourke, Glastonbury, and the Natural refuge at Castle Brent. I revealed my parents' true identity and that I was Aldrich's niece. I did my best to recount the true story of the cataclysm and how the rift had been torn apart when Arthur and Lancelot crossed swords over Guinevere. I told him about Gilhana and her prism and meeting the Lady of the Lake.

Then I told him I was Arondight.

He listened in silence, allowing me to get everything out. When I was finally done, I tensed at his silence.

"I knew it," he whispered. "I knew there was more to you."

"How? The thought never crossed my mind. When I went to see the Lady of the Lake, I thought I was going to die. Instead… I'm not sure if it's a blessing or a curse."

"A blessing, Purples," he stated.

"Wilder—"

"It's okay."

"No, it's not. What you did to that demon…" I shook my head. I was about to turn his entire life on its head, but something told me he already knew what power lingered inside him. All he needed was to hear the words. "Wilder, you're Excalibur. You're the Argent Flame."

He stared at me, his expression blank. I hated when he did that—when he kept his cards so close I couldn't see them.

Then he grunted.

"Is that all you have to say?" I whispered.

"What am I supposed to do about it? I have the soul of a celestial being wrapped around my Natural soul in a strange symbiosis no one can explain. I still don't know where I came from. Knowing I'm the lost reincarnation of a bloody sword hasn't changed anything for me, Purples. You…you were born to this. Me? I was ostracised by my own people because they thought I was part demon, and now I'm bloody Excalibur?"

"The sword was just the vessel," I murmured lamely.

"And you're Arondight."

I nodded.

"Bloody hell." He sat up and pinched the bridge of his nose, screwing his eyes shut. "So, what is this thing? All I can feel is liquid fire inside me. It burns unbearably. My veins… I turned that greater demon into ash with my bare hands." He fisted his fingers into his hair and tugged. "There's something in my head and I don't know who it is. I'm not alone and all I feel is *rage*. Burning, fiery, *rage*. I want to tear the world apart, Scarlett. I—"

I felt the flame inside him stir and I grasped his face in my hands. Leaning my forehead against his, I rubbed my thumbs back and forth across his flushed cheeks. He wasn't wrong when he said he felt like he was on fire.

"It's going to be okay," I murmured. "I'm going to help you."

"How? I don't know what I'm supposed to do. I don't know *how* I'm supposed to be." His cheeks were damp.

"Twin Flames," I whispered. "Remember how our Light joined together? Remember how you helped me destroy Markzoth? We can only be better together."

Wilder sighed and placed his hands over mine. "Now I know why I went into that pub."

"*8-bit?*" I asked. "I thought you were tracking a demon."

"I never saw it until I went inside."

Could it be? Had our souls known who we were

even before we did? This world was becoming more twisted and full of coincidences which were turning out to predestined meetings the longer I was in it. Scarlett Ravenwood had started out as a little girl on the run, then an angsty teenager struggling with the foster system and mental illness, and finally, becoming the saviour of the bloody world. What was next?

Wilder tugged my hands away from his face and we sat together for a while, content to let everything that'd happened sink in.

After a while, he asked, "How long was I in that house?"

"Four months, give or take."

"Four months?"

"I was gone for six. And FYI, I would never have put that coin into that stupid rock if I'd known it was going to fling me back into the Middle Ages."

"*Hell.*" He leaned back against the wall. "Does Greer and Aldrich know you're back? Jackson? We have to go back to the Sanctum."

"Uh… they know," I said carefully.

Wilder tensed and studied me with his silver eyes. I guess he got the eyeballs and I got the hair. I couldn't imagine him with grey hair, though men like him seemed to become even more handsome the older they got. *Lucky bastard.*

"What aren't you telling me?" I held onto a sudden swell of tears and he grasped my hand. "*Scarlett.*"

I took a deep breath. He'd find out soon enough,

though I wish it didn't have to be now. Finding out he was half Excalibur was burden enough.

"Please," he whispered. "What's wrong?"

Then I broke the news about our current state of affairs.

"We took out the alpha site, but it was a trap," I told him. "It was too easy. We were ambushed once we got inside, but it was like they weren't even trying. It wasn't until we returned to the Sanctum that we realised the demons' true intentions."

"The Sanctum?" Wilder asked, his eyes wide.

"It fell," I whispered. "Berlin, Rome, New York, Sydney, Los Angeles… We don't know how many more. They were all destroyed in one coordinated attack led by—" Memories of human features emerging from a twisted construct of black essence— the sharp line of a jaw, angled cheekbones, muscled arms, ivory flesh made new—it surfaced like a long-lost nightmare, though it only happened a week ago.

Wilder tugged only hand, his flame brushing against mine. "By who?"

I looked at him, my heart heavy. "Mordred."

"Mordred?"

"Arthur and Guinevere's son. When Camelot fell, they took her captive and used her in their experiments. Mordred…well, he's the first incarnation of Human Convergence."

"And he's in control of the Sanctum…and the city, I suppose." He sighed sharply. "I don't know what to say. All of this—"

"You don't have to say anything if you don't want to."

"The Codex?"

"I went back in and got it. I had to. Greer said she's connected to it and if the Dark found a way to possess its power, they could use it to track down every living Natural."

"You went into—" He bit his tongue.

"I wasn't strong enough to fight him. It was all I could do to get away with the Codex." I lowered my gaze. "I lost everything that meant something to me that night—Galahad's letter, your troll doll, my mother's arondight blade… I barely escaped with my life."

"Where is it now? Where are the others? Greer—"

I hissed and tugged my hand away. Excalibur and Arondight must come together in love…but it all seemed like such a farce when he spoke her name. I knew they'd parted ways, but it still stung. Romantic love joining with the love of a friend? I wasn't sure it was compatible enough to close a rift between parallel universes.

"Purples…"

"Aldrich took what survivors he could to a safe place. I don't know where it is, and we haven't heard from them since that night."

"We?"

"Jackson and Esme are here," I explained. "They pulled me out of the Thames and saved the Codex from sinking to the bottom." I snorted and shook my head. "It's the cataclysm all over again."

"And now we're supposed to fight?" He rose to his feet and began to pace. "I don't understand this thing inside me. I don't know how to use it. All I feel is *fire*. You know, all of this seemed achievable when we were looking for a bloody sword," he seethed. "There wasn't any pressure on me to be a saviour. I mean, what a twist, huh? The Natural everyone hated is now the only thing that stands in the way of total world destruction?"

"Not the *only* thing." I rose to my feet and slammed my palm against his chest, stopping him in his tracks. "Now you know how I feel."

"Do you feel this same uncontrollable—" He pursed his lips and thumped his fist against his sternum. "I feel like I'm going to tear apart at any second."

He went to push me away, but I stepped into him, leaning my cheek against the crook of his neck. Snaking my arms around him, I held him close and listened to the wild thrum of his heartbeat. I'd never held him like this before and it was electrifying. It was intoxicating—holding someone in my arms who I cared about so deeply—and I never wanted to let him go. It didn't seem to matter that his feelings were unknown to me, but I knew they would the moment my embrace broke.

"The night you left…what I said to you was true," he told me. "I don't know how I feel, Scarlett. I don't want to hurt your feelings, but how is keeping that from you fair?"

And so, the world would burn. I swallowed my disappointment and pulled away, masking it before he saw it in my expression.

How could I tell him about the Lady of the Lake's revelation? I couldn't. It would likely be the final push that broke Wilder entirely. When I lost control of Arondight with hate in my heart, I literally exploded. Who knew what Wilder would do.

"Forget about all that," I said. "We're safe, that's all that matters right now."

"But we're not, are we?"

"We have a moment to breathe," I whispered. "So, let's just—"

"Scarlett…"

I lifted my head and met his gaze. There was something different about the way he looked at me, and I wasn't sure if it had something to do with his awakening or his new perception of me as Arondight. Whatever it was, I finally felt as if he saw me as his equal.

I smiled, my heart warming. "I'm still trying to figure this thing out, but I'll help you, Wilder. We'll do this together."

"Twin Flames," he murmured.

I let it settle in for a moment, then I asked, "Are you hungry? There's a lifetime supply of dinosaur-shaped spaghetti in the kitchen."

11

———

Hunger drove us to the kitchen.

"Hey, you're up," Jackson exclaimed as we appeared. "You want something to eat? Dinosaur spaghetti?"

Wilder glared at him and sat at the table; Esme hesitated as she stirred a pot of something on the stove.

Jackson glanced at me and I frowned, not liking where this was going. I mean, I didn't expect Wilder to just accept everything that I'd told him, but he was much more adjusted than I was. His reaction worried me.

"I see you've told him," Jackson said to me.

"She told me," Wilder stated, looking at Esme, who was turning beetroot red under the force of his stare. "I took it well."

"As well as a kick in the balls," I said, sitting across from him.

"I need a moment," he snapped. "I know we don't have time, but *bloody hell*."

I grimaced and turned my head away.

Awkward silence fell over our little group and we listened to the clunk and hiss of the boiler firing up downstairs. A moment later, the radiator rattled as it began to heat the chilly little kitchen. Too bad it couldn't warm up the frosty mood everyone was in.

Without warning, Wilder jerked to his feet, making my heart leap, and stormed out of the room.

I listened to his footsteps on the stairs and knew he was going to the roof. He liked being up high. I supposed it isolated him from the noise he'd had to put up with from the world. Strangely, I'd found the same kind of comfort in it.

"I should probably give him a moment…" I said.

I knew what he'd be going through up there. Looking across a city awash with colour, he'd be in overload. When I came back, I was expecting to be different. I never knew how, but I was prepared for the change—but Wilder wasn't. He'd been slapped with it out of nowhere and the trauma he'd been through last night… I just couldn't fathom it.

"So it wasn't the reunion you were hoping for?" Jackson asked with his brow cocked.

I shook my head. "Not exactly."

"It's a lot," he said, echoing my thoughts. "I thought demon hunting mages were pretty out there, but this… Well, this is out there even for demon hunting mages."

"Having your identity change overnight isn't

something easily handled," Esme added. "We all know what that's like." Except Wilder now had the extra pressure of being one half of the flame which was supposed to save the world. "And given the current state of things…"

"And he tried to kill you," Jackson added.

I scowled. "I don't think he remembers that."

I leaned back in the chair and worried my fingernails with my teeth—a bad habit I hadn't turned to for years. We were in a bad position. The Naturals were scattered, Mordred and his band of demons were taking control of the city and hunting us down, we had the Codex, Greer and Aldrich were out there some place, and Wilder and I had to get a handle on our powers and fix the rift before it was too late. We had a fifty-fifty shot, but that was only if we could get to Camelot in the first place.

Esme set a bowl of dinosaur spaghetti down in front of me and I stared at the little t-rexes floating amongst the brontosauruses.

Whatever we did next relied on Wilder. A man who'd been ostracised, abandoned, had his heart broken, and who's very being had been stripped away from him—and we had no time.

The upstairs bedroom was a mess. Jackson had strewn his things everywhere and it was a feat considering he only owned the clothes on his back.

I could see Wilder sitting outside in the dark, his

shoulders hunched inside his coat. I opened the window and climbed out onto the roof, the cold air blasting my cheeks. I huddled into my jacket and steadied myself on the slippery tiles.

Wilder's head was buried against his knees as if he was trying to hide from sensory overload. I sat next to him and looked out over the city. It was like a Technicolour aurora when Arondight decided to look through my eyes. It was strange—I was Arondight, but I also felt like it was a separate identity living alongside Scarlett. What did I call myself? Scardight? Aronlett? I snorted and looked at Wilder.

"I figured out that all those funky lights are people's auras," I said quietly. "If you look close enough, you can tell the demons from the humans. Naturals look just like humans, though."

"It's too bright," he said, his voice muffled.

"An unbelievable amount of people are crammed into this city. Seeing them all makes me wonder how they stand it."

He raised his head and looked at me, squinting as if he was trying to block out some light.

"You get used to it," I said slowly. "I've learned how to turn down the intensity."

"I keep seeing things," he said. "Echoes of things I did when my soul was gone." Well that doesn't sound good.

"It wasn't you," I told him. "How could it be when what makes you *you* was gone? Bodies retain echoes. The brain is a mysterious thing, you know."

"You're different," he murmured.

I smirked. "So are you."

He remained tight-lipped, which was completely out of character. Usually, he was the one doing the counselling, not me.

"We've become who we were always destined to be," I said, trying to be the voice of reason. "Life happened and we evolved to cope with it."

"Complete with a terrible legacy." Wilder snorted. "We tore open the way between worlds and we're the only ones who can repair it."

"We didn't tear open anything," I told him. "Arthur and Lancelot were the ones who wielded our power when it was inside their swords. It wasn't our doing."

"Our Natural souls give life to beings with no identity of their own."

"Something like that. I barely understand it myself."

"I assume the rift is in Camelot," he went on, "…wherever that is. Yet another thing we've lost."

"Galahad told me where it is. We don't have to worry about that part at least."

Wilder tensed and closed his eyes. "You talk about Galahad like you cared about him."

"Of course, I did," I said. "He helped me find my way back."

"I didn't mean it like that."

I shrugged. "Arondight was bound to his bloodline. Whatever he felt beyond friendship was an echo of that."

Wilder grunted and turned back to the city. "Do you know what the colours mean?"

"Nice segue."

"I've got a lot of information to absorb, Purples. And having a psychedelic headache isn't helping."

"I know. I've been there. As for the colours, I have no idea. I suppose they mean something, but stuffed if I know."

"Am I still Wilder?" he asked quietly. "Am I still the same man I was before Excalibur took hold?"

"Yes, you are," I replied. "The only thing that's different about us is that we are *aware*. I'm still Scarlett and you're still Wilder. We just have access to *more*."

"It sounds so simple when you put it that way."

"Because it is, Wilder. This power was always inside of us, shaping who we've become. It was just… sleeping and now it's awake." I took his hand and reached out to him with my Light. His sliver flame stirred within, reacting to the swirl of its twin.

"I understand now why our Light kept wanting to join," Wilder murmured.

"I don't know what will happen if we combine completely, but a little seems to be okay for now."

He grunted, letting me know he got it. Together we had enough juice to rip apart space and time.

"I'll get you another troll doll," he promised.

I laughed softly, tightening my grip. "I'll hold you to that."

After a while, I left Wilder to his thoughts on the roof and ventured inside. I blew warm air on my hands as I went downstairs, and my ears pricked up as I heard Jackson and Esme's raised voices echoing down the hall.

When I poked my head into the kitchen, I was surprised to see Esme talking excitedly on the mobile phone, her hands waving in the air.

"What's going on?" I asked with a frown. She was so animated I was having a hard time deciphering what she was saying.

"It's Aldrich," Jackson said with a grin. "We finally got a hold of him."

My eyebrows rose. "What? How?"

"I had his number from before," Esme said to me.

"Why didn't you call him before?" I demanded. "And how does everyone get a mobile except me?"

"I've been trying," she explained, "but it hasn't connected until now." She listed to something on the other end of the line and then handed the phone to me. "He wants to talk to you."

I snatched it from her and pressed it to my ear, my heart almost bursting. "Aldrich!" I choked.

"Scarlett?"

"*I found him*. I've found Wilder."

"Thank the Light," he said with a sigh. "That's the most reassuring thing I've heard in a long time."

"Did Romy find you?" I asked. "Has anyone else…?"

"She did," he replied. "We've gathered a number

of us together, but we can't stay here for long. Madeleine is here, I thought you'd want to know."

"Thank goodness!" I exclaimed, my heart leaping. "I'm glad she's okay, but you have to know what I found in the Sanctum. Aldrich…"

"What is it?"

"There was a greater demon there, though he revealed his true self to be a Natural twisted by Human Convergence."

"A Natural?"

"We all wondered what had happened to Guinevere after the cataclysm, but she was captured by the demons and used in their experiments." I looked at Jackson and Esme, who were looking anywhere but at me. I couldn't blame them. "The demon I faced was Mordred, Aldrich… He's Arthur and Guinevere's son."

He hissed, the sound cracking over the phone. "The oppressive demonic essence with the glowing red eyes? We've seen him, too."

"You have?"

"Yes. We didn't engage. I knew there was something about him…"

"Good. Even I wasn't enough to fight him."

"Listen, Scarlett, we need to get out of the city. It's not safe for us here. We're going to find a place where we can assemble and plan our next move. I want you to join us."

I tensed. There was only one place left in the world where I knew we'd be safe—that's if it was still standing. After all, eight hundred years was a long time. Greater structures had fallen is less.

"Aldrich, when I was in the past, the Naturals had a safe haven in the west called Castle Brent. They took refuge there in the years after the cataclysm. It was an ancient site that had been built on a place of power. The Light there had been woven over centuries and the demons or humans didn't know about it. For all they knew, it was the site of an Iron Age hill fort."

"Castle Brent?" he asked. "Do you think it still stands?"

"I hope so, because it would be the only place left in the world Mordred wouldn't be able to touch. Galahad told me it only showed itself to those in need, and we really need it right about now."

"Brent... Brent Knoll. Just south of Bristol." The phone rustled and he spoke to someone in the background. "We'll find it, Scarlett, but what about you?"

"I have to help Wilder," I told him. "His awakening wasn't easy... I'm going to send Jackson and Esme to meet you. They have the Codex."

"You saved the Codex?" His voice rose. "Greer will be relived."

I looked up as Wilder came into the kitchen, his gaze shifting to the phone in my hand. "Is she there? I think Wilder wants to talk to her."

"Hang on..." There was a rustling on the other end and I held out the phone to Wilder.

He stared at me curiously, taking the mobile from me with gentle fingers.

"Greer," he said, not even attempting to break his gaze from mine. I didn't know what he was trying to say to me, but I didn't like the way it made me feel.

I turned, giving him some privacy and filtered his conversation out. There were some things I didn't need to hear.

"You're sending us away?" Jackson demanded. "Why? We can't just leave you here."

"You have to," I told him. "The Codex won't be safe here, and Mordred will find the house eventually. If he gets his hands on that book, we're screwed."

"Then why aren't you coming with us?"

"I have to stay behind and help Wilder. Being at the centre of a war council won't help him figure out all the stuff I dumped on him. We need time alone so I can help him with his abilities. Besides, it's better if Wilder and I are nowhere near the Codex."

"She's right," Esme said. "We can't help them, and the Codex needs to be protected. It's best if we meet the others at Castle Brent."

"We'll join you soon, no doubt," I added, overly conscious of Wilder standing behind me. "When we're ready, we'll have to go to Camelot." Whenever that was.

"Galahad told you where to find, right?"

I nodded. "It's on the other side of the country. Brent is closer to it than London."

"To think it's been hidden all this time," Esme mused. "I wonder what's left?"

"Nothing good," I stated, glancing up as Wilder handed me the phone.

"Greer," he said.

I nodded and pressed the phone to my ear once more. "Greer? What's up?"

"Scarlett…" She sounded worried and lost for words—two things the protector rarely was.

"He'll be fine," I told her. "And the Codex will be back with you soon."

"Have you told him?"

I tensed. Wilder was watching me, and Jackson and Esme were discussing how to get out of London. I turned away and rolled my eyes. "It's not that simple."

"I trust you'll do the right thing."

"Of course, I will. I almost blew up half a city block the other night. I know what's at stake."

"You—"

"Okay, okay, it was just a quarter."

"Scarlett, I meant it when I said I trusted you, but this—"

"Isn't something I can force, Greer. You and I both found that out the hard way."

"Just…just don't underestimate him, okay?"

I could feel his gaze burning into my back. "I never have."

Her sigh echoed down the line and I looked over my shoulder at Wilder.

"Don't worry, Greer," I said, raising my voice. "We'll all be together soon. I promise."

"Castle Brent?"

"That's the one."

"Scarlett?"

I bristled and tightened my grip around the phone. "Yeah?"

"May the Light be with you."

A smile tugged at my lips and I began to warm a little towards her. "And you."

12

It wasn't one of my finer moments, but the next thing I did was steal a car. We'd planned out their route last night and at first light, I hot-wired some random's car with my mind. Now I was a vandal *and* a thief, but Wilder was the one who'd suggested masking the licence plate with an illusion.

"How will we let you know we're safe?" Jackson asked as they put the bundled-up Codex in the backseat.

"We won't be far behind," Wilder replied as I hugged Esme.

"He's still cocky," Jackson said to me. "He thinks he can get a handle on being full superhero that quickly?"

"You know I'm standing right here," he drawled.

"Oh shush yourselves," Esme scolded. "We've got a long drive ahead of us. At least we're going against the morning traffic."

"Always the optimist," I told her with a smile.

She hugged me again. "Take care."

As soon as she'd let go, Jackson wound his arms around me. "I know you'll be fine, but hurry back to us, okay?"

"You worry like an anxious parent," I said, my voice muffled.

"Someone has to."

"You better get moving," Wilder said. "The longer we're out here, the more likely we'll be spotted."

Jackson pulled back and gave me a look.

I made a face. "I thought you were over that."

"You're my best friend. I'll always look out for you, no matter how many superpowers you get."

I laughed and shoved him towards the car. "Stay safe, okay?"

He grinned and slid into the driver's seat and Esme slipped into the front beside him.

As they drove away, I was keenly aware that Wilder and I were alone. Someone had always been with us—Jackson, a horde of demons, humanity. Even when we'd been training, there'd always been someone not too far away. Now we were on our own and we were Twin Flames—irrevocably connected on a spiritual level I was yet to understand.

All I wanted to do was wrap myself around him and never let go—which could be construed as adorable *or* creepy, not to mention totally cringe worthy.

We went back into the house, the cloak taking us into its illusion and hiding us from the world. I knew Jackson and Esme would be okay. Their demon mutations would mask them from the Dark long enough to get the Codex out of London and to Brent. Besides, Jackson was definitely not the same nerdy gamer geek I used to know.

"I think we need a drink." Wilder opened the fridge, took out a six pack of beer, and set it on the table.

"Where did you get that?" I exclaimed grabbing the bottle.

"You found my weapons, but you didn't find the beer?"

"I've never been a big drinker, but I could use one today."

He watched as I sifted through the drawers looking for a bottle opener. "Priorities?"

I grunted. "Where the hell is the bottle opener?"

"You don't need pointless kitchen appliances when you're a Natural." He pressed his front against my back and I stilled, my heart skipping a beat, and he placed his hand over the top of the bottle. There was a hiss as he opened it.

"Call me old-fashioned, I guess," I murmured as he tossed the cap into the sink.

I didn't know if I should turn around or not. If I did, then he'd be within kissing distance and I was so bloody confused. One twist of my waist and there'd be a total lip graze.

I thought about the time he'd kissed me in the hall outside my room at the Sanctum and promptly turned to jelly. All he had to do was give me a look and I'd fling myself at him, but I was too afraid to turn around. If he said the same thing to me about not knowing how he felt, then that'd be the third time. Everyone knew if you said the same thing three times in a row your wish would come true. Maybe that was just a fairy tale, but I wasn't in the mood for more risks.

"I'm stronger today," Wilder said, moving away. "I get what you mean about turning down the intensity."

"I forget you had more training in Light Studies than I did." I tightened my grip around the bottle of beer and turned to face him.

His lips quirked. "You were the one who aced your classes in mere months. It's a little insulting, really."

I snorted and puffed out my chest. "I had a good teacher."

"You mean Masters? I seem to recall you threw him across the room with your mind on the first day."

"I wasn't referring to Masters," I said with a pout. "I was talking about you."

"Way to stroke my ego, Purples."

"Glad to see you're feeling better."

Wilder snorted and looked out the window at the overgrown garden beyond. "You were born to it. I understand it now."

"So were you."

"It seems so." He grabbed a chair and set it against the radiator, then put another beside it. Sitting, he patted the space beside him.

I sat, shivering as I realised how close he'd positioned my chair to his.

"Cold?" he asked.

"This house is drafty as," I declared. "You're not really into home maintenance, are you?"

His gaze burned into the side of my face and I squirmed. "Not really. I'm much better with swords than hammers."

I felt my cheeks heat, and I sipped my beer to hide my embarrassment because my mind went straight to the gutter. I made a face as the liquid hit my tongue, the taste unfamiliar after so long without drinking—not that I'd been big on it in the first place. I was much more interested in the sweater side of things—cider with pear, apple, or berries, that's what I preferred. I'd think of any random thing to take my mind off my sexual attraction right about now.

"How did we become what we are?" Wilder wondered out loud. "Did the Lady of the Lake ever explain it to you?"

"Not really," I replied, thankful for the change of subject. "She was vague about a lot of things. From what I understand, my parents were chosen. It wasn't a bloodline thing, or reincarnation, or whatever. I am my parents' biological daughter, but who knows how the rest happened. It must have been divine intervention."

"Sounds creepy."

I rolled my eyes. "Look who's talking."

"I've been wondering about that," he murmured, picking at the label on his beer. "If my real parents were killed like yours," he snorted and shook his head, "would they have left me otherwise? Was knowing what I was too much for them? Or did they not have a choice?"

My heart swelled and I studied his features. He looked sad, as if he was on the verge of losing it. He'd been through a lot in the last few days so I couldn't blame him. Regaining his soul and awakening as Excalibur was traumatic at best, and then there was all the rest.

"You don't even know who they might've been?" I asked.

"No."

I was lucky then. I knew who my mother and father were and even had a surviving family member in Aldrich. But Wilder had nothing.

"I remember flashes of a life, but nothing solid until I was nine or ten," he said, "when I went to the Academy. I was an orphan then, with no family to go back to."

He'd told me about his time at the Academy in fleeting sentences. When holidays rolled around, he'd stay behind and train because there was no place for him to go. With his differing abilities and looks, he was an outcast even then. It was all he'd known.

"There were teachers who seemed to care, but I was just one of many students," he went on. "There was always a caretaker and a few staff members during holiday periods, so I was never totally alone."

"It must have been awful."

"No. I preferred it." He shifted in his chair and looked at me, his gaze raking across my features. "What was it like for you? In all those foster homes?"

I shrugged. "Some were okay, most weren't. School was the hardest part. It sucked always being the new kid, especially when I looked different."

His lips quirked. "Your hair?"

"I didn't exactly meet uniform standards." I snorted and turned the beer bottle around in my hands. "I had a foster mum who tried to dye it once. It never took and no one could figure out why."

"Magic," Wilder said.

Yeah, magic. It was easy to dwell on what if's and not do anything about the what now. It was a trap I'd fallen into a lot growing up, but hopefully, that lesson could help with the darkness that awaited us outside the safe house.

"I was angry a lot," I said quietly. "I had dreams about my parents, though I didn't understand them. I knew they'd been murdered, but no one would ever talk about it. I was assigned councillors, but they were so jaded by the system, they either didn't care or didn't know how to help. So I became angrier and lashed out a lot."

"You had no one to tell you who you really were," Wilder murmured.

"I never finished high school, you know. The Academy was the only place I ever got a certificate."

"Really? I don't believe you."

I clinked my beer against his. "I remember I'd been called into the principal's office. He gave me a lacklustre speech about how I was ruining my life, then when I left, Sally Mathewson was in the hall and gave me some serious lip."

"Sally Mathewson?"

"The nasty so-and-so who made it her life's work to ruin mine. She laid into me with her venomous tongue and I punched her in the face."

"Can't say I'm surprised with your response," Wilder stated.

I grunted and took a sip of beer. "I had my fist in the air ready to punch her again when the principal threatened me with expulsion."

"What did you do? Did you hit her?"

"No." I shook my head and sighed. "I walked out and never looked back."

Wilder leaned back, resting his head against the wall. "Kids suck."

"I'll say."

We sat in silence, contemplating the things we'd learned about one another. Wilder knew so little about who he was and where he'd come from, it hurt my heart just thinking about it. Perhaps in time, the flashes of his childhood would awake in his dreams like some of my memories had. Now that Excalibur had awoken, maybe it would help him.

"You're my family now, Scarlett," he declared out of nowhere.

Great. Family said a lot about my romantic prospects. "We're not related, you know."

He laughed and downed the rest of his beer. "I know that. It's a philosophical thing."

"Cool."

He cocked an eyebrow. "Cool?"

"If I'm going to get stuck with someone, it may as well be you."

He grinned. "Charming."

I felt Arondight stir, itching to come forth and explore. With Wilder here, it seemed to want to be present more often.

"I can feel it," he stated. "I'm…aware."

"You can tell when Arondight…"

He nodded. "I need to learn about Excalibur," he went on. "We're meant to use our power for the Light, but I have no idea what it can do."

I coughed and looked at my hands. I had to tell him about the love thing eventually, but I wasn't sure how to bring it up.

"What?" he asked.

"Just make sure to use it with pure intentions," I told him.

"What does that mean?"

I shrugged. "It was just something the Lady of the Lake mentioned. It seemed important."

"Pure intentions?"

I shrugged again and took the beer bottle from his hands and handed him mine. "You want the rest of this? I can't finish it."

He gave me a look that said he wasn't convinced I was telling him the whole story, but that was Wilder—he always knew when I was being shifty. He took the beer anyway, letting the unsaid remain that way for now.

"There's got to be more Naturals out there," I

said. "They'll need our help. It'll be on-the-job training for both of us."

"There weren't many of us to begin with," he mused. "Barely a hundred."

"There's no telling how many are lost, how many are with Aldrich, and how many are…" I let the end of the sentence hang in the air, unable to finish it. "How many are scattered across the UK?"

Wilder shrugged. "Aldrich would probably know, but when the Sanctum fell, they'd know not to come here. They have protocols to follow."

"Need to know," I muttered, wishing we had something harder than beer. In this weather, I could do whiskey.

"We can find them now," Wilder went on. "Anyone who is still trapped in the city, we can help them get to Castle Brent. Then we can join the others and figure out what to do about the rift."

"What about Mordred? If we cross paths with him—"

"We fight, Purples. It's what we've trained for. Protecting the Light from the Dark."

"You're so well adjusted it makes my head hurt," I drawled.

Wilder grunted and picked at the label on his beer bottle. "It's the only thing I know how to do."

"Fight?"

He nodded. "I've been doing it my whole life."

13

We didn't waste any time. Once it became dark, we ventured out into enemy territory, searching for lost allies in the chaos.

Wilder walked beside me, the collar of his leather biker jacket flipped up with a matching black woollen scarf knotted around his neck. It felt like old times, stalking the city together in search of a demonic threat cloaked from the human world by our Light.

"It's quiet," I murmured as we sidestepped a group of young men headed towards a pub. "I thought there'd be more activity."

"They have a more concentrated game now that they have us on the run," Wilder replied. "I don't think they realise that the both of us are aware now. Perhaps that's our one saving grace."

I grunted, picking up on the subtle differences in his demeanour. Since I'd found him in the Grey Lady's house and returned his soul, Wilder seemed older somehow. Perhaps older wasn't the right word. Maybe wiser? Yeah, wiser.

"I wonder why it's flame," I mused.

"Maybe it's because it's the way you picture your ability in your mind," Wilder mused. "We've always been told about the flame. Stories have power."

"Then where does the liquid fire come from?"

He shrugged. "I felt sick to my stomach when my soul reentered my body."

"You're saying you were manifesting liquid flame because your soul was throwing up?"

He raised an eyebrow. "Stranger things have happened."

We reached the street corner and stopped, watching the flow of humans going in and out of Camden Town tube station. It was ironic that we found ourselves back here given our history. The Stables market wasn't far, and opposite was the newer markets where *8-bit* was nestled inside. We'd come so far since that first night—my twenty-fifth birthday.

I edged closer to him, more for comfort than warmth. The air shimmered with more than the aura of the population. The ice crystals of an incoming frost were gathering, making the air heavy with moisture.

"Give it a try," I said. "See if you can pick up on anything."

Wilder nodded and I assumed he was giving it a red-hot go, but there was no way of telling. He was squinting ready hard, if that was any indication.

Sighing, I joined in his citywide scan, my mind

soaring above as we lingered on the street. It wasn't long before I felt something out of the ordinary, but it wasn't hard these days.

"Can you feel that?"

Wilder nodded. "A concentrated spot of demonic activity. More than usual."

Usual meant one or two Infernals hanging out together stalking some unwary prey. Lesser demons liked to horde together like a swarm of zombies, but this was a deeper infestation.

I threaded my arm through his and we hovered together in the stars above. If I blinked, I could see through my Natural eyes, but all it did was make me dizzy.

Wilder hissed, "They're gathering an army of possessed humans against us."

"Mordred," I said. "It has to be." Using the people we were sworn to protect against us was a low blow. "If Mordred controls the Infernals, does that mean that if we kill him, then they will be freed?"

"Seems logical," Wilder replied then tensed.

"What is it?"

"Do you see that?" he asked. "There's two bright sparks amongst the Dark. They've faded but… *There*."

I gasped as I saw a flare of Light emerge from the Darkness. One spot, then two.

"There are Naturals there," I exclaimed. "Can you make out where in the city they are?"

"Hold on." He tugged on my hand, drawing me back to our bodies. "I want to try something."

I yelped as he grabbed me around the waist and

propelled us into the air with Excalibur. Wind tore past my face, making my eyes water something fierce and tearing away my foul-mouthed complaints before I could hurl them at him.

Just as abruptly as he'd taken off, we landed in a gust of metallic-tasting wind that made me gag.

"Show off," I said, gasping.

"You've never tried that?"

"I jumped out of the Sanctum when I did a snatch and grab of the Codex. Somehow, I landed in the Thames." I *hmphed* as I remembered Jackson telling me that I'd flown. How I'd done it was another thing entirely.

Wilder rolled his eyes. "I wonder how that happened."

I patted him on the shoulder and made a face. "Eyes on the prize. We're in the swamp now, buddy."

"Buddy?" He tilted his head to the side. "I was expecting you to say something witty about us being able to fly, but now I'm just disappointed."

"And the cocky Wilder returns." I screwed up my nose and turned towards the gooey wad of demonic activity. Why hadn't I tried to fly before? I was kicking myself.

We made our way towards the Light that'd brought us here, aware that whoever was trapped amongst the concentrated Darkness was in a whole heap of shite.

"What's the game plan here?" I whispered.

"We get the Naturals to safety," Wilder murmured. "Engaging a demonic army when we're still trying to control unknown powers would be a terrible idea. We get them out and excise any possession."

The air rippled before us and I grabbed Wilder's arm, pulling him back. "Wait."

Movement stirred and he glanced at me. "I didn't think this would be so easy."

"Yeah, because it's not."

"We have to stop meeting them like this," Wilder drawled.

"That's our fault. You and I are just a pair of arrogant risk takers."

"Look who's talking. You're the one who constantly runs headfirst into dangerous situations."

"I'm an indigo magnet. What's your excuse?"

Wilder grunted and reached for his arondight blade.

There were two of them. They prowled though the shadows towards us and the tang of Dark was unmistakable.

"Naturals," he whispered.

"I saw this at the Sanctum. Naturals possessed with infected Infernals."

"What happened to them?"

"I was able to push the Infernals out of their bodies with Arondight."

"That's reassuring. That exorcism rite is way too wordy, you know."

"*Don't I ever.*"

"You talk a lot when you get nervous."

"Better than doing a nervous poo." I stepped towards the two Naturals. "Stop right there!"

"We knew you'd come, but him?" Martin prowled out of the shadows, the streetlights illuminating his hollow face.

"Martin?" I held my breath, shocked to see him trapped by the Dark. If anyone could've escaped its grasp the night the Sanctum fell, it was him.

A flash of red drew my gaze to the woman behind him and I began to raise my hand. *Valeria*.

"They're bait, Purples," Wilder whispered.

"We can't leave them," I hissed. Arondight stirred inside me and my palm heated. "I'm getting those Infernals out."

"Agreed. You better show me how it's done, then."

I pushed my Light outwards and a burst of indigo flame slammed into the Naturals. The flame lit them from the inside, burning away the Infernals who were possessing their bodies.

Valeria gagged, her gaze finding mine. "Scarlett?

I sighed in relief and went to meet them, but Wilder grasped my arm. "*Wait.*"

Martin prowled towards us, his lips curving into a malicious grin as his arm rose.

"*No,*" I cried.

I felt his Light stir and his aura sparked with tiny bolts of red lightning. The Dark controlled him so fully that the mutation had seeped into his soul. That's why my flame couldn't burn away the corruption. The only person who could help him now was Ramona… and I didn't know if she'd made it out of the Sanctum.

Valeria took a step towards us, her face pale. "Scarlett, I'm stuck—"

"You had to come out of your hole sooner or later," Martin said. "And when you did, we'd be waiting."

He grabbed Valeria and caged her against his chest with his left arm and pressed his arondight blade against her throat. "Put your swords down," he snarled.

Valeria cried out as he jerked her closer, his lips moving against the shell of her ear. I could see the fear in her eyes and the shimmer in her aura as her hope began to fade.

"It's over," Martin said. "The end has come for the Naturals, and the time of the Dark is rising." His eyes filled with inky blackness as he was overtaken by the demonic force inside him, and he slid his arondight blade across Valeria's throat.

I screamed as she fell to the ground, blood gushing from her opened flesh, and lunged.

Wilder grabbed my arm and pulled me back. "Scarlett, no," he said, holding me against his chest. "It's what Mordred wants. We can't harm our own."

I looked down at Valeria and my heart broke as I

thought of Alo. How could I tell him that the woman he loved was dead?

Martin laughed and ground his boot into her side. He'd never do that if he was free. It was too late… Mordred had complete control over him.

"You know he's gone," Martin said. "He's *evolved*."

"Mutated," I snarled, my hand wrapped around Wilder's wrist. "There's a difference."

"You have to learn who holds the power here, Arondight," he said, the sinister smile fading from his features. "It's only a matter of time before the Light will be snuffed out." He raised his hand, holding out his bloodied arondight blade. "*This world is ours.*"

His sword sparked and in a burst of silver Light, the hilt spun out of his hand and he stepped forwards. I gasped, turning away as the blade severed his neck. Wilder's hand buried into my hair as he held me close, his flame simmering.

"Don't look," he whispered. "I've got you."

"How *charming*."

My blood chilled as the abrasive rasp of Mordred Pendragon echoed around us. I pulled away from Wilder's grasp and turned to face him with a snarl.

He'd put on his best face for the occasion, his swirling cloak of Darkness fell over his human-like shoulders, and his eyes were nothing but pits of glowing red that reminded me of congealed blood. His armour was a glistening black plate and chainmail with a sword hanging at his waist.

Flame crackled as he left smouldering ash behind him, his footprints burning the ground. His smooth features shimmered, revealing his true form underneath—a ruin of twisted flesh and bone. Human Convergence had ravaged his Natural body beyond recognition. The armour was real enough, but his face was only a vain illusion.

"I saw you made short work of the Grey Lady," he declared, his hand curling around the hilt of his sword. "Impressive, but we all know no Natural has enough power to take out a creature like her."

Wilder tensed beside me.

"She was a Druid once, you know," Mordred continued. "We took her on a hillside where she waited for us—a willing sacrifice."

I gasped as I realised he meant the Grey Lady was the twisted remains of Philomena, Gilhana's sister. "*No.*"

Darkness radiated off him in sickening waves as his lips twisted. "Oh yes. We couldn't turn her into a demon, but she became the next best thing."

"She still had enough sense to defy you," Wilder snarled.

"Oh is that so?" Mordred drawled. "If she didn't, then we wouldn't be one step closer to merging our two worlds…*Excalibur.*"

I took Wilder's hand and let my Light call out to him. I had to erase the hate from my heart so we could stop Mordred without giving him exactly what he wanted.

He couldn't help what he was…he was made this way. His future had been taken from him before he was even born. This life was all he knew. War was a terrible burden for both sides.

Demons were just living up to their true nature. It wasn't personal.

"Pure intentions," I murmured.

Wilder squeezed my hand, letting me know he understood.

Mordred snarled, unsheathing his sword. "You dare defy me?"

"What did you think we were going to do?" I drawled. "Cower like frightened animals?"

"We're the Twin Flames," Wilder declared. "We exist to fight arseholes like you."

Mordred's cloak flared behind him as he called on his Darkness and his human body dissolved while his demonic essence boiled forth.

We called on our flames, silver reaching for indigo, but Mordred had anticipated it.

His sword slashed between us, forcing Wilder and I apart. I spun, my arondight blade sparking to life as Wilder did the same. We moved in unison, like reflections in a mirror.

Mordred would try to keep us apart to save his own skin—he knew the flames couldn't merge or he was toast. Together, Wilder and I were at our full strength, the power of the heavens no match for the Darkness from another world—and that's what made us so dangerous.

Mordred slammed the hilt of his sword into Wilder's head, opening a jagged gash in his flesh. Remembering Galahad's lessons, I cried out and swung my blade at the weak spot at the demon's knees. Steel bit through flesh and his leg collapsed beneath him. He landed hard, his armour clanking against the ground.

Wilder reached for me. "Scarlett!"

I grasped his hand and the moment we touched, the Argent Flame wrapped around Arondight and I jerked awake, my body erupting in Indigo Flame. We merged, the flame licking along my skin, leaping out to entwine with the iridescent fire which engulfed Wilder.

I didn't know where I ended and Wilder began. Arondight had taken over and Excalibur had answered the call, turning their wrath onto the unnatural abomination bearing down on us.

We lunged, colliding with Mordred so hard we hurtled across the street and slammed into the building opposite. Masonry shifted and rumbled with the impact as our hands wrapped around his throat.

Were they mine, or Wilder's? Or were they both?

Mordred screamed, his voice tearing apart as his body, burning from within, began to disintegrate. The ground shook, the paved footpath cracking as we channelled our energy into the demon's destruction.

With one last cry, he burst apart in a gust of black smoke, what remained of him dissipating in the frigid air.

Wilder and I twisted apart, the fire ebbing to a slow simmer inside me. I gasped for breath, not understanding what we'd just done.

Ash fell around us like snow, settling on our shoulders and hair, forming drifts on the ground. Wilder's gaze met mine and I breathed heavily as I watched the gash on his forehead disappear, the flesh knitting together in an accelerated time-lapse.

My gaze lowered, raking over his features, and I felt a zap of electricity surge through my body. It hit all the right places and I began to tremble. We'd merged and the world hadn't imploded. The rift was as it was, and the power that'd flowed through us had been intoxicating. Our true nature was laid bare and everything I was, Wilder had seen. Nothing was hidden from him now. He'd seen my heart, but I'd also seen his.

My fickle humanity almost made me shy away. I turned to face him, but he'd already taken me in his arms. He kissed me, his mouth covering mine, his heart beating so hard I could feel it thrum through his chest as I melted into his grasp.

I buried my hands in his hair and held him to me, the taste of him strangely metallic.

"Pure intentions," he murmured, his lips rough against mine. "I gathered it meant this."

"Wilder—"

He kissed me again, my words lost until he managed to tear himself away.

"It's okay. I know why you didn't tell me." His fingers traced the curve of my cheek, his chest heaving. "It had to be true."

"I was afraid. I—" I swallowed hard, grasping at his jacket.

"I didn't know. I-I didn't understand." His grip tightened. "I was torn in so many directions I couldn't see, but now I'm *awake*."

"Is it because of what I am?" I whispered, tears stinging my eyes.

"No," he replied firmly. "I saw you, Scarlett…all of you. I saw it even before I knew I was Excalibur."

I shook, holding onto him for dear life. "You felt it, too?"

"We both know our truth now." He cupped my face in his hands. "You saw into my soul and you still want me."

"How do you know?" I teased, my heart easing.

"If you didn't, would you have kissed me like that? It was indecent."

"Still a smart-arse, I see."

His lips curved upwards. "Do you realise what we just did?"

I frowned, awareness of the world around us flooding back. The street was covered in ash, scorch marks burned onto the side of the surrounding buildings, and the footpath was cracked. Not to mention the damage we'd done to the wall beside us.

"We merged, Purples," her declared. "We merged and the world is still here."

He was right, which meant we had a real chance of closing the rift without making it apocalyptic.

I snorted. "Yeah, but who's going to clean up this mess?"

14

Naturals that had fallen in the field were given to the elements.

It was a tradition Wilder taught me that night and the first I'd heard of it. Until Galahad and I had parted at the standing stones, I hadn't suffered the death of a friend like I had Martin and Valeria.

The city was under siege and nowhere was safe. We couldn't even be certain the Academy or the catacombs under Glastonbury were secure. There was no other recourse but to scatter their ashes and offer them back to the Earth they'd fought so hard to protect.

In the aftermath, London had gone Dark.

We looked out across the city with Alexandra Palace behind us. From on top of the hill, we had a panoramic view of London and her surrounds. It was the perfect spot to survey the auras flitting about below, but the stark absence of anything Natural was glaring.

"There are no more," I said, burying my hands into my pockets. I closed my fist around the ring I'd plucked from Valeria's finger and thought about Alo. Martin hadn't been wearing anything for us to take back to his family, but Wilder had their arondight blades. It was something, at least.

"Did we kill him?" I whispered. "Did we kill Mordred?"

Wilder shook his head. "I doubt it."

I shivered, imagining Mordred out there some place, attempting to reconstruct his body. It wouldn't be as grotesque as a greater demon, but it was still unsettling. At least the human army he'd been gathering had been freed from their possession. Like the Naturals, I couldn't sense the concentration of Infernal activity anymore.

"If we close the rift, he won't go away," he stated. "None of the demons who remain here will."

I looked at Wilder, knowing our greatest battle wouldn't end the stranglehold the Dark had on our world entirely. Cut off from their power, they'd likely fade as they'd done over the past eight hundred years, but they wouldn't go without a fight.

"Wilder…"

He turned and slid his hands over my waist, his gentle demeanour almost too good to be true.

"We have to go to Castle Brent," he said. "London is gone."

"For now."

He pulled me into his arms, attempting to soothe me, but the gesture was alien despite our feelings for each other. Wilder and I had come together, but it was bittersweet in the aftermath of our battle with Mordred.

"There was nothing we could do," he murmured. "Martin was consumed by Human Convergence. It'd taken his soul."

"I know."

"The Grey Lady was raising her own army," he said. "We put a stop to both, but Mordred will start again."

"If he comes back," I said, knowing it was wishful thinking. Demons like him had an annoying knack for regenerating.

"If he does, then we'll make sure to put him down for good. Once the rift is closed, we're going to take back our home."

"Sounds like a vow."

"That's because it is."

"I never heard you refer to the Sanctum as home before."

"It's the closest thing I've ever had to one," he said with a shrug. "More so now that you're here."

I grunted. "You know, if we weren't demon hunting mages with celestial beings wrapped around our souls, I would think you're coming on way too strong and break up with you."

He laughed softly. "It's strange. I feel…"

"You were always so hostile and standoffish," I told him. "The only time we touched was when we trained."

"Was it?" He *hmphed* and stroked his fingers through my hair. "I never noticed."

"That's such a male thing to say."

"Does it matter? I'm here now."

I narrowed my eyes. "Do I have to worry about the force of your passion the moment we're alone and not hunted by demons?"

"Of all the things I thought you'd say to me, '*the force of your passion*' was not one of them."

My cheeks flushed and I turned away, scanning the hillside. Below, a row of houses flanked the park. Cars lined the entire street, just waiting for me to choose one to hot-wire with my mind.

"Scarlett—"

"We need to find a getaway vehicle," I interrupted. "If we leave now, we could get to Castle Brent by sunrise."

We went to the street below and walked along the line of cars. It didn't sit well having to steal again, but I wasn't sure we could fly all the way across the country, let alone have enough ID and cash to rent a car. As I flipped the lock on a grey sedan at the end of the row, I hoped the owners had full comprehensive insurance.

I was content to let Wilder drive, so I settled back and stashed Martin and Valeria's arondight blades in the glove box for safekeeping. My hand lingered on the hilts, the memory of Valeria falling to her knees flashing in my mind.

"Okay?" Wilder asked as he clipped his seatbelt into the buckle.

I slammed the compartment closed. "Okay."

He didn't look convinced, but he let it go, concentrating on navigating us out of the built-up residential area of North London to the M4 in the west.

"How long has it been since you slept?" Wilder asked, easing the car onto the nearly empty motorway.

"Don't know. I wasn't tired until you asked me."

"It's about a four-hour drive. I don't know what we'll find when we get to the castle, so I'd grab some sleep while you can."

"What about you?"

"You know me, Purples." He flashed me a wicked grin. "I've got stamina for days."

I snorted and made myself comfortable. "You talk a big game, Excalibur. I hope you can live up to it."

It felt like I'd just closed my eyes when I was nudged awake.

"Huh?" I mumbled. "What's wrong?"

"We're being followed."

Blinking, I looked over my shoulder at the single pair of headlights behind us. I could feel the zap of red energy and sighed.

"It's a pair of greater demons," Wilder stated.

"They really pulled out the all stops for us, didn't they? I'm flattered, really."

"We can't lead them to the others."

I leaned forwards and peered into the side mirror. The headlights shone behind us, keeping a steady pace on the empty motorway. Wilder was right—we had to shake our tail A.S.A.P.

"Did I ever tell you about the time I fought a fresh demon on the back of a speeding horse?" I declared.

"I don't know which of those things to ask you to explain first," Wilder said, checking the mirrors.

I unclipped my seatbelt and began to climb into the backseat. "A car isn't exactly a horse, but I can work with it."

"Hey," Wilder exclaimed. "What are you doing?"

"What does it look like?"

I slipped into the backseat and rolled down the window. Icy air blasted inside the cabin, whipping my hair in all directions. I stuck my head outside and began to clamber out.

"Scarlett, I don't—"

I didn't hear what Wilder said next. I grabbed hold of the roof of the car, kicking my legs up onto the edge of the window. If anyone was driving in the opposite direction, who knows what they would've thought seeing a woman hanging off the edge of a fast-moving car. They'd probably call the police on us.

The demons behind us began to speed up, and I didn't waste any time. When I'd done this before, I'd had a straight shot right off Weston Super Mare's butt, but I was slightly off centre. It didn't matter—I had an internal course corrector on board.

Not thinking twice about it, I jumped.

I felt weightless as I hurtled through the air, the

demon-mobile rushing towards me. I hoped I'd judged the distance correctly, but it was too late for do-overs.

I landed on the bonnet, my feet leaving deep indents in the metal. The force of my landing sent the nose downward and almost flipped the car. I leaned forwards, my arondight blade sparking to life before I rammed it through the windshield.

There was a crack of glass and a roar of pain from inside. *Bullseye.* I allowed the blade to sheath, using my free hand to wrench the shattered glass away. The two male demons stared at me in shock for a split-second before they sprang into action.

The car swerved violently to the right as the driver attempted to dislodge me, but I was stuck fast. Who needed magnetised boots when you had Light, huh?

The passenger didn't seem to notice he had a stab wound through his chest as he lunged for me, but all he got was a kick in the face for his troubles.

Light seared through me as I slid feet-first through the open windshield and in-between the two demons.

"Hey, boys," I said as I slammed my hands down onto both of their throats.

Indigo flame poured out of me and into the demons, their shrieks cut off as they exploded. Their heads went *pop*, then they went *poof* as they turned into man-sized fireballs. Heat seared my skin as the driverless car clipped the guard rail at the side of the motorway, then flipped into the air.

I was tossed over and over, a loose projectile in a tin can. My head slammed against the roof and my body flung back and forth, but I didn't feel a thing. I knew I totally would afterwards, but after I'd healed myself the night I'd fought soulless Wilder, I knew this was nothing in comparison.

When the car finally came to a rest, I lay in the wreck, listening to the click of the engine as it cut off and began to cool. The stench of leaking petrol and oil filled my nose, mingling with the rank sulphur scent the greater demons had left behind. Putrid farts, the both of them.

"Scarlett!" Wilder roared as he skidded down the embankment. "*Scarlett!*"

I pulled myself out of the twisted metal, the cuts and scrapes already fading to nothing before I had a chance to feel them. It seemed my adrenaline still worked. Next time I'd have to think about exit strategies.

My boots squelched in the muddy ditch as I walked towards Wilder, the remains of Indigo Flame ebbing through my limbs. It was intoxicating and I knew if I let it, it would overwhelm me and who knew what'd happen then.

He grasped my face, his thumbs rubbing at the blood. "Are you okay?"

"Piece of cake," I declared.

"Are you bloody crazy?" he demanded. "What were you thinking?"

"Don't underestimate the element of surprise," I said with a grin.

"*Purples.* I thought you'd—" He clamped his mouth shut and shook his head. "You're crazy, you know that?" He looked over my shoulder at the twisted wreck and frowned.

"They're gone," I told him.

"Two greater demons? Just like that?" He snapped his fingers mockingly.

I nodded. "Just like that."

He looked down at me, his eyes flashing silver in the half light. "You walked away from something that should've killed you."

"I noticed." I cracked my neck. "I've had worse though."

"What are we?" he whispered.

He felt it, too. The wild, unnamable flame we shared burned just as brightly in him as it did me. We knew the stakes by now, but Wilder was still new to it.

"Death, life, destruction, passion," I murmured. "We mustn't forget."

The sun was a sliver on the horizon when we reached the tiny village of Brent Knoll in the county of Somerset.

We left the car a few miles outside the village and walked through the dawn towards the hill fort. The landscape was different and little remained of what I remembered from my first visit here.

"Are you sure it's here?" Wilder asked, his voice muffled by the dense air.

We passed a church, the headstones of the cemetery rising ominously out of the mist.

"It's built-up more than it used to be, obviously," I replied as we turned off the land and onto the trail leading up to the hill fort.

Fences and narrow roads wove through the fields, the marks of human habitation littered everywhere. A thick frost had fallen during the night and ice coated every available surface. It dripped off wire fencing, crystals formed on blades of grass, and I felt it in the air with every breath I took. Even the tip of my nose was numb, and I rubbed it before it froze solid. Our boots crunched on the trail and I craned my neck, searching for my first glimpse of the last refuge of the Naturals in Britain.

As we broke through the trees, I paused as the sky shimmered. The veil around the castle was still there, hiding the fortress from human eyes. It lingered in a place between this world and the next, just like Avalon had.

As we climbed the rise, it began to emerge from the ancient power woven into the stone.

"That's the castle Galahad took you to?" Wilder's voice was loud in the silence.

"The one and the same."

"How doesn't anyone walk into it?" Wilder mused. "It's nothing like any cloak I've ever seen."

"Magic," I told him.

He smiled. "Fancy that."

I grinned, glad to be back in familiar territory. The yellow banners were long gone and one of the towers was crumbling, but it was still Castle Brent.

A thread of smoke rose upwards into the sky from

within the walls and shadows moved on top of the battlements. We'd been spotted. Someone was here and I hoped Aldrich had been able to gather the survivors without too much fuss.

"This is your mighty castle?" Wilder asked, peering up at the ragged tower.

"Nothing lasts forever," I said, hoping it wasn't an omen of things to come. "C'mon, let's see who's here."

15

———

Shouting echoed over the wall of Castle Brent as we walked up the path.

The portcullis was shut tight, the mechanism likely rusted with time. We were forced to slip through an opening that'd been reserved for guards and messengers to get inside the grounds.

People emerged from within the inner fortress, bleary-eyed and hopeful the new arrivals would be their loved ones. It broke my heart to see their disappointment when they realised it was just Wilder and me standing in the muddy courtyard.

Greer walked towards us, a relieved smile on her face, but it wasn't Wilder she was excited to see. She threw her arms around my neck and held me tightly as if I might disappear at any moment. I could feel her Light simmer as she swallowed her tears.

I was frozen, unsure if I should hug her back.

"Thank you," she whispered into my ear. "Thank you for saving the Codex."

"It was my duty."

Pulling back, she looked me in the eye and said, "No, it wasn't. You walked into utter devastation to save us all." She took a deep breath and squeezed me tighter. "You didn't even hesitate. After all this time, my biggest regret was not trusting you the moment Wilder brought you into the Sanctum for the first time."

I scoffed, untangling myself from her embrace, "Life's too short for regrets, Greer."

She smiled, her gaze flickering to Wilder. "Yes, you're right."

Aldrich stepped forward, drawing my attention and she stepped away to greet Wilder.

"We searched for the others," I said.

"But you came alone," Aldrich murmured.

"I'm sorry." A barrage of *what ifs* tumbled through my mind. What if I'd gone out looking earlier? What if I'd left Wilder to rest and searched then? What if we'd been a few minutes earlier, would we have been in time to free Martin?

Aldrich grasped my arm. "Scarlett, this was going to happen with or without Arondight and Excalibur."

"How do you know?" I whispered. "We've lost so much. I lost Andromeda's arondight blade and—"

"It doesn't matter," he said, interrupting me. "Beating yourself up over things you can't change is useless. Think of what we have to face next. We have the Twin Flames and with you both here, we have a chance for a future. Memory is nothing if we aren't here to remember it. Don't fret about Mea's blade. You're more important."

I swallowed my brewing tears and nodded. He was right, and in that moment, I was glad to have someone like him in my life—*my uncle*.

"How many made it?"

He lowered his gaze. "Less than fifty from London."

A pang tore through my heart. "Is that all? What about the outposts? The Academy? Glastonbury?"

"Islington and the other teachers managed to get the students to safety, but it's only a temporary refuge. Some parents and family are with them, too. They're considering coming here, but we're unsure if that's a wise decision." He took in the assembling Naturals and lowered his voice. "We need to talk, but later."

I nodded. Talking about our dire circumstances would only sow the seeds of panic. "I assume Jackson and Esme made it here safely."

"They're inside. Ramona put them to work in the infirmary the moment they arrived. She set it up in the hall inside."

"Ramona made it?" I sighed in relief. "Thank God."

"You and Wilder should get some rest. I think we should meet this evening to discuss further steps."

"Agreed." I clapped him on the shoulder.

"And Scarlett…your arrival has given us hope."

Despite myself, I smiled. While there was a chance, those around me could see a future. It was a heavy burden, but one I could face with Wilder by my side.

"Who is it?" A desperate voice echoed across the courtyard and I let go of Aldrich, turning to look. "Valeria? Is it Valeria?"

Alo.

He broke through the crowd, his eyes shifting from me to Wilder and back again. "Scarlett?"

My breath was shaky, and I took Valeria's twin arondight blades from Wilder.

"*No...*" Alo began to shake, his eyes full of disbelief.

"I'm sorry, Alo. I'm so sorry." I slipped the hilts into his big hands as tears fell down his cheeks and soaked his beard.

"Did she— Did she suffer?"

"No. It was merciful."

"Merciful." He snorted and shook his head, his grip tightening around the hilts.

Everyone was staring at us, watching our exchange with sombre expressions. They'd hold their loved ones a little more tightly tonight, and those that'd lost would hold Alo in their arms.

I looked around at the crowd and they bowed their heads in a silent vigil, the rising winter sun casting a sombre glow across their shoulders.

"Scarlett?" Romy's voice echoed across the courtyard as she jostled through the Naturals. "Scarlett?"

Shifting nervously, I glanced at Wilder. Martin had been Romy's partner for better or worse. No matter his arrogant and abrasive nature, they were still close. They'd fought side-by-side since leaving the Academy, and that left a mark which could never be erased.

She emerged from between two Naturals and hesitated when she saw Alo holding Valeria's arondight blades. Her gaze took in his anguish and she turned to me and Wilder, resignation in her features. It was as if she'd been expecting bad news.

Wilder stood before her and held out Martin's arondight blade.

She took the hilt and held it against her heart. "Martin, he…"

"He was infected," Wilder said. "I'm sorry, but there was nothing we could do."

She choked back a shocked gasp and blinked furiously.

"We were hoping you could keep his blade for his family," he added.

Romy nodded, unable to stop her tears. "He fought for the Light…and he died for it. So did Valeria. We know this may be our fate, but we bear arms despite it."

"For the Light!" someone shouted.

"*For the Light*," the assembled Naturals echoed.

Aldrich and Greer had done quite the number on the crumbling castle.

There was no electricity or running water, but the

Naturals had made the most of it. The kitchen was up and running, a fire burning twenty-four-seven in the giant hearth. The dining hall had been turned into a makeshift infirmary. The tapestries had been taken down and beaten free of dust, every corner of the room swept and washed, and furniture had been repurposed into beds for the ill and injured.

I was looking for something to eat, more than some place to sleep, when I heard my name being called. "Scarlett!"

I cried out as I was almost flattened by Madeleine. She threw herself into my arms and held on like a barnacle at the bottom of a boat.

"You made it!" I embraced the young girl, holding on a little too tight myself.

"Thanks to Ramona," she explained.

"Your parents?" I asked.

She shook her head. "I haven't heard anything."

"I'm sorry."

"It's okay. A lot of people have lost their entire family. There's a chance they're at an outpost someplace or with the others from the Academy."

"How are you? How is things going with your—" I waved my hands.

"My mutation?" She shrugged. "Ramona says I still have Light, but I can't feel it."

"Oh, Madeleine…"

"It's okay. At least I'm still on the right side, huh?"

I smiled and as if on cue, my stomach growled. "Want to find something to eat? There's no way I can sleep at a time like this."

The kitchen smelt like noodles and musty dirt when we walked in. It was a heady combination, but I was too hungry to care what else was growing in here.

Someone had managed to scrape together some chicken noodle soup—the source of the smell—and we found a spot by the hearth and slurped to our hearts' content.

That's where Jackson found us.

"I can't say I'm surprised you found the food so quickly," he said, sitting beside Madeleine.

"Do you want some privacy?" the girl asked, looking between us.

"It's cool," I replied.

"I don't mind. I have stuff to do anyway," she said with a shrug. "Ramona's got a whole list of things that need to be done."

"She's right," Jackson said. "We're trying to set up a mobile lab so we can at least make some progress on all that stuff we found at the alpha site."

"Ramona thinks she might be able to make a vaccine," Madeleine told me.

I raised my eyebrows. "A vaccine?"

"Yeah, it'd prevent people from getting infected in the first place."

It made sense. We'd destroyed their lab, but there were still Infernals out there who carried the infection. It wouldn't do much for the humans, but at least we'd be able to fight without compromising ourselves.

Madeleine took the empty bowl from my hands and stood. "I'll see you later?"

"Probably. I'm not going anywhere anytime soon."

"That depends on what Aldrich and Greer have to say in their super-secret meeting tonight," Jackson stated.

I snorted. "It's not so secret if everyone already knows about it."

He laughed and pushed to his feet. "C'mon, I wanna check out the view from up top. I haven't had a chance yet."

Thankful for the distraction, I followed my best friend out of the kitchen and through the castle. We passed Naturals busy with various duties, some of them new faces. There were more than fifty people here, so word had gotten out to the others.

I could see why Aldrich was hesitant to allow the students form the Academy to come here. There wasn't enough to go around as it was, and more bodies meant a larger footprint we might not be able to conceal from the world. The last thing we needed right now was disclosure.

I climbed the stairs leading to the top of the battlements with Jackson bringing up the rear. At the top, I spotted a Natural at the other corner, sitting on the remains of the crumbing tower with a pair of binoculars.

The day had dawned bright and the sky was blue, though it hardly fooled anyone—it was as cold as the North Pole. Mist clung to the countryside, frost lay thick on the grass, and my breath vaporised in dense, white plumes.

"I never saw the view from up here," I said, looking down the hill to the village below. "I suspect it's a little different anyway."

"No roads or cars," Jackson mused.

"Far from it."

Remembering Bedivere and the other knights of Camelot, I smiled and picked at a clump of moss growing in a crack in the stonework. I'd hardly had time to know them, but I'd always remember them—especially Bedivere, despite his involvement in the Order of the Twin Flames. All their meddling and Gilhana's prism had brought me here for the second time, though the simple life seemed farther from my grasp.

"So…you and Wilder, huh?"

I felt my cheeks heat and I dropped the moss over the edge of the battlements. "You picked up on that?"

"Why are you so embarrassed? Isn't it a good thing?"

I shrugged. "I'm just hoping it's not too good to be true."

"That's the pressure talking." He draped his arm over my shoulders and pulled me close. "If you took away all that other stuff, you'd be grinning like a fool."

"You didn't have any trouble getting out of London?" I asked.

"Smooth, Ravenwood. Real smooth."

"Did you?"

"No. Our ride was smooth as a baby's bum."

"So much smoothness."

"The strangest thing happened last night,

though," he said. "I was slapped with the most abrupt hangover. Sick to my stomach, a raging headache, dehydrated—the whole thing. All the hybrids felt it…"

I turned to face him and his arm fell away. "You were all sick? No one else?"

He nodded. "Yeah. At first I thought it was something we'd eaten but no one else seemed to have it."

Could it be Human Convergence? Wilder and I had blown Mordred into vapour…

"*Shite*. Mordred," I murmured.

"Mordred?"

"Wilder and I fought him last night." I shook my head, not liking what I was suspecting. "He lured us out and we had to merge to take him down."

"You merged with Wilder and the world didn't end?"

Jackson hadn't come to the same conclusion I had, and I sighed. Always with the terrible choices, huh?

"Mordred is the first incarnation of Human Convergence," I stated. "Everything that came after, came from him."

"You think we're linked because of it?" He grunted and rubbed his eyes. "Seems obvious now that you mention it. We all felt sick at the same time."

"We're not sure if he's dead, Jackson."

"Which is probably why we're still alive."

I didn't know what to say about that. I bet he was wishing he was at some e-sports tournament right about now. Those things were cutthroat, but not on the same level as demonic invasions from a parallel universe.

"We can't let a piece of shite like that roam around," he added. "I guess biting the dust is a small price to pay…"

"You can't mean that!"

"We're talking about the fate of the world, Scarlett," he said. "If he's in your way and you have the chance, don't hesitate."

"Even if it means your life?"

"Like I said, it's a small price to pay." He smiled and bumped his shoulder against mine. "After all the adventures we've had together, I've had a good life. I've seen a world not many have had the chance to see. And I've known love."

He turned his back on the view and gazed down at the courtyard where Esme was rushing around. She was looking for someone—Jackson.

"There's no way of telling if you're connected that closely," I argued. "It might be nothing but a psychic connection, not a physical one. If it were physical, he'd know where you are. Remember how you could see Markzoth?"

He frowned. "Yeah. Maybe you're right."

"Have you tried to connect with anything since then?"

He shook his head. "Seemed too risky."

"Has anyone else?"

"The council forbade it, so I assume not."

Below, Esme had spotted us and was waving her hands. "Scarlett! Aldrich's looking for you!"

I grunted and waved down to her to let her know I'd heard. To Jackson, I grumbled, "Duty calls."

"It's a bit early for your secret meeting."

"I guess word's spread that I don't need sleep."

"When *was* the last time you slept?"

"Can't remember. Sad, huh?" I thought about it for a moment, then added, "I did get a few minutes in the car on the way here."

"That's not the same thing, super freak." Jackson smirked and nudged me towards the stairs. "Go hatch your plans for saving the world. And give Wilder a kiss for me, huh?"

I rolled my eyes, but I couldn't help but grin at him.

"There's the smile I was waiting to see."

The audience chamber wasn't quite as I had remembered it, but it held echoes of the knights of Camelot.

The same worn table was in the centre of the room, though time had ravaged it even further. The fireplace was built into the wall at one side, the hearth cracking with a blazing fire which lit the room. The chandelier still hung from the centre of the roof, but it was covered in cobwebs and all the candles were missing. Light filtered through the arrow slits in the walls, though the windows had been covered to keep out the chill.

Wilder stood by the fireplace warming his hands while Aldrich bent over a map on the table.

I stood by the hearth, my arm pressing against Wilder's "You didn't sleep, did you?"

"You didn't either," he murmured.

I pouted. "How do you know?"

"You really have to ask me that? I know where you are, Purples. You shine like the bloody North Star, you know."

"That's romantic." I pinched his arm. "Did you know the North Star is called Polaris?"

He smiled down at me and shrugged. "If you say so."

Footsteps echoed behind us and we turned to see Greer walk into the room with the Codex in her arms. It was strange to see the book outside of the conservatory, but this was where its life began under the pen—or was it the quill?—of Sir Percival.

"Good, we're all here," she said, placing the Codex onto the table.

"Isn't anyone else coming?" I asked.

"The fewer people who know our plans, the better," Aldrich replied. "We trust our own people, but we're going to discuss how to save this world. There's only going to be once chance."

"And we can't take any unnecessary risks," Wilder added.

"Galahad showed you the location of Camelot, didn't he?" Aldrich asked.

I closed my eyes and recalled the vision Galahad had shown me. We'd soared across the countryside, over moors, valleys, and forests. Over water, castles, and villages until I'd seen the gash that'd torn the world apart. A great castle split in two, covered in Darkness, the battlements crawling with inky back demons.

"It's to the north of here, though the landscape has changed. Humans have built over so much of it." I looked down at the map and traced my figures north of Castle Brent. "I want to say it's here, just above Ludlow."

"Shropshire," Aldrich mused. "Lovely place."

"You've been?"

He nodded. "When I was much younger, though if Camelot is there, it's well hidden."

"Darkness controls the area," Wilder said. "If they don't want us to find it, we never will."

"You could've said the same thing about the Necropolis," I argued. "But we found that just fine."

"There was historical record of it. Camelot is a myth," he replied. "If you listen to the stories humans have cooked up about our heritage, they'd have it clear across the country in Sterling."

"It doesn't matter," I fired back. "I trust Galahad, and I trust that Arondight and Excalibur will help reveal it to us. It's our fate to go back there."

Greer and Aldrich were watching our exchange like it was a tennis match.

"They won't let us just walk in the front door," Wilder went on.

"No. I suspect it'll be twisted somehow. Full of traps."

"The moment they know we're there, they'll throw everything at us. The more we know, the better off we'll be."

"I'm not arguing with you. I totally agree."

"We'll scout the area first. Make sure we can get in unseen."

"They've been expecting us for eight hundred years, Wilder. There is no getting in unseen."

"Do you want us to leave?" Greer asked.

I held my tongue and flushed as Wilder coughed loudly.

"What is the Codex's wisdom on the topic?" he asked, bowing his head.

"There is no wisdom it could impart," she replied, placing her palm on the cover. The air rippled around it, the book appearing happy to be in its birthplace once again. "We have entered a new age where new pages are waiting to be written."

"Well, it's the perfect place for a writer's retreat," I told her. "This was where the Codex was born."

Greer looked at me with unmasked interest.

"Sir Percival began to work on it here in the years after the cataclysm," I added. "When I was here, he had just begun." I leaned across the table and placed my hand in the cover. "It's happy to be home."

"Sometimes you give me chills, Scarlett," Aldrich said, glancing at Wilder.

"I believe I've been trying to tell you that ever since I found her in that nerdy pub," he drawled.

I shook my head and turned towards the fire. "When do you think we should strike at the rift?"

"I propose in a week's time," Aldrich replied. "It will give us time to verify the location of Camelot and scout it's perimeter."

"If you know what to expect of their defences, it will give you both the best chance," Greer said, clearly in agreement.

"A week is too long," Wilder argued. "It's barely been a week since I awoke, and we've already lost so much. If we wait, then we risk losing everything."

"And you want to rush in there wielding a power you hardly know anything about?" Greer argued. "One chance, Wilder. *One chance* at stopping this."

Aldrich grunted, clearly not impressed. "What do you say, Scarlett?"

I watched the flames crackle and pop, the scent of wood smoke thick in the air. "I think we should get in there as soon as possible…but not before we've had a chance to prepare."

Wilder snorted, the sound echoing in the cavernous space. Without the tapestries on the walls, sound just bounced to its hearts' content in here.

"That's an uncharacteristic opinion for someone so fond of asking questions after the fact," he stated.

I turned and glared at him. "We're talking about the fate of the entire world, Wilder."

He grasped my forearm. "I know."

"You'd have us leave in five minutes!"

He pulled me close, forgetting we had an audience. "You can't tell me you didn't feel what I did when we merged, Scarlett. The *certainty*."

Greer gasped. "You merged?"

"We wait," I murmured. "At least until we know, *without a doubt*, where Camelot is. It's not like you can go without me."

Wilder's lip curled.

I sighed. Fighting with him the last thing I wanted to do. "Relationships suck, huh?"

"Now I know why I avoided them for so long."

"Do you ever have the feeling you're a third and fourth wheel?" Aldrich said to Greer.

She laughed. "There may as well be no council at all."

"It would have been easier with swords," he added. "Don't you think?"

"Yes, I agree. Swords don't talk back."

16

___

Bedivere's smithy was empty when I finally had a chance to linger.

I wasn't sure if the meeting was a success or not. Wilder had his own wild ideas, Aldrich had been as sensible as ever, and Greer had no insight whatsoever. She was right about one thing—we were in uncharted territory, and as far as anyone knew, no one had been back to Camelot since the night of the cataclysm.

I stood beside the anvil and imagined Bedivere forging the first arondight blade. My own felt heavy in my pocket, but the loss of my mother's weighed heavier. Who knew things would have turned out like this? Did Andromeda and Chris know my destiny would have led me here? The cruel thing was, I'd never know.

There'd been so many losses, so many lives taken, all to bring us back to this point—a place we'd been before.

I knew I'd have to risk my life, but if I'd known

the world would come right to the brink…? Honestly, I don't know what I would've done. This was the hand we'd been dealt and now we had to play it to the end.

"Bedivere's forge," Wilder said, his voice comforting. It wasn't surprising he'd found me here, but I was glad for his company.

"He had the hots for Gilhana," I told him conspiratorially. "I think she had them for him, too."

"The druidess? The old woman who used to clip me on the ear when I forgot her chocolate bars? Are we talking about the same person here?"

I laughed softly. "Yeah, the one and the same."

He moved closer, his boots crunching on the rocky earthen floor.

"I think we should go tomorrow," he said. "There's no advantage in waiting."

"Tomorrow?" I turned with a frown. "And not tell anyone?"

"It's safer that way."

"Are you sure?"

"I know you think it's reckless, but we have no time."

"You said it yourself, you awoke barely a week ago and before that, your soul was trapped in a jar for months."

"I don't remember it." He took a step towards me and Arondight flared. "And how long has it been since you were awoken? A month? It takes most Naturals a lifetime to reach their full potential, but we aren't Naturals anymore, Purples."

I shook my head, knowing he was right. We were

something else—something that didn't have a name or a place to call home. The Lady of the Lake was gone, though I wasn't even sure she understood where her people had arrived from. Celestials—that's what the demons kept calling us.

"You do that a lot lately," Wilder said.

"Do what?"

"Lose yourself in your thoughts," he replied. "What aren't you saying?"

"There's so many strings attached to this power," I murmured. "So many things could go wrong."

"What strings? We've been just fine. We merged and lived to tell the tale, Purples."

I still felt like it'd been a fluke. "When I lost control of my power back in London, it was because I had hate in my heart."

"Hate?"

"For what the demons had done to us." I ran my fingers over the anvil, the rough metal cool to the touch. "You know what jealousy did to the world. Can you imagine what hate could do?"

Wilder sucked in a sharp breath and I knew he understood what I was getting at. Pure intentions were a thinly veiled attempt at concealing the truth of our merge. We got lucky when we faced Mordred, but we couldn't count on it happening twice.

"Why didn't you tell me?" he whispered.

"What difference would it have made?" I asked,

turning to face him. "I can't force you to feel anything. I—"

He was standing right behind me, his presence tugging at my heart. "*Scarlett.*"

"We have to merge with *love*," I said. "We have to feel the same thing at the same time or it won't work."

"And you're afraid I don't feel the same for you as you do for me?" He ran his hand over his face, his palm scratching against the stubble on his jaw. "Purples…"

"Maybe it's my own insecurities talking, or maybe it's the constant reminder of you and Greer—"

"Greer and I were never meant to be," he interrupted. "That was my fickle human heart. For all the power we had as Naturals, we were still human at our core, Scarlett. Who has power over love? *No one.*"

Foolishness washed over me. He was everything I'd ever wanted—if we were just plain old humans, I'd still feel the same—but I was my own worst enemy.

His fingers were warm in mine and I felt his power stir. "Merging will be no problem."

I looked up at him, my heart jack hammering in my chest.

"What I feel for you is something deeper than love," he told me. "But if you want to call it that, I guess that's what it is." He took a deep breath, his eyes shining silver in the lengthening shadows. "I love you, Scarlett."

My humanity told me I should have been afraid of losing myself in this thing with Wilder, but what we were transcended knowing. When we merged, we were one and identity didn't matter. Wherever we'd come from, it was a different way of life than we'd known growing up as human or Natural.

I leaned into him, my fingers tracing the sharp curve of his jaw until I buried them into his hair. My heart thrummed a wild tempo and my tongue felt thick. Why was it so hard to say those three little words? I'd said them about him before, but not *to* him. I felt them deeply—as deep as he'd confessed—so why were they stuck?

"It's because you haven't said it before," he whispered, his gaze searching mine. "Because the world has shown you nothing but bitter disappointment. I'm sorry to have put you through what I did, Scarlett. But—"

I kissed him, partly to shut him up, but mostly because it was the only thing I wanted to do for the rest of my life. How he knew my heart was beyond me, but so was everything we managed to do in the past week.

I'd barely pulled away before I blurted, "I love you, Wilder."

"When this is over, we'll have all the time in the world." His lips brushed against mine, sealing the promise.

"Tomorrow," I breathed. "I can't believe we're going so soon."

"There's no time, Purples, but I hear you loud and clear."

"Are you sure you're going to be okay?"

He nodded. "I have to be. It's only been a few days since you found me in that house, but I've never felt more *myself* before."

I wrapped my arms around him and nestled against his chest, his warmth seeping into mine. I could feel Excalibur stir and I closed my eyes, listening to it.

"This feels so final," I whispered.

"This is not the end, Purples… It's only the beginning."

I hoped he was right.

His lips found mine and we kissed, the Twin Flames stirring as our touch intensified. There were at least a dozen dirty jokes in there about merging, but I was too far gone to think of one. After wanting him for so long, it felt as if I was going to explode.

"Come to bed," I rasped.

His eyes sparkled. "Bed?"

"This is what people do the night before a battle, you know."

"Is that right?" he hissed through his teeth as my hand moved into the indecent zone. "*Purples…*"

"No matter what happens tomorrow, I want to have you every way I can." I breathed deeply, my body trembling under his touch, as his did mine. "Merge with me, Wilder."

"Merge with you?" He grinned, his embrace deepening. "*Gladly.*"

17

The following morning, Wilder and I left Castle Brent in secret.

We ventured north, following the vision Galahad had given me in Avalon. I hoped the others wouldn't be too angry with us, but this was something Wilder and I had to do on our own.

We had nothing else to go on but a gauge marking on a map, so we began our search in Shropshire. The Clee hills were nestled in a part of the countryside which was littered with Medieval heritage. Old castles and hill forts dating back thousands of years dotted the landscape. There were plenty of nooks and crannies to hide a tear in space and time.

The closer we came to the hills north of Ludlow, the darker the sky seemed to become. Either the demons knew we were coming, or one hell of a storm was brewing.

"It's here," Wilder said as we parked the car.

We'd picked up the one we'd left outside the

village near Brent instead of rousing the whole Natural encampment—which was would have happened if we'd tried to nick one from there.

"How do you know?"

"We created the rift, Purples. Or at least, our power did. It's like a homing beacon just activated." He pointed. "See?"

I squinted at the view and it began to change like one of those *Magic Eye* puzzles. "Optical illusions at their finest."

I got out of the car and slammed the door, assessing the fence at the side of the road. We'd have to climb over and go up the hills…or between them. Camelot was somewhere in there, or at least, the outer edges of what was left.

Wilder's boots crunched on gravel as he appeared beside me. "Up and over, Purples. It's time to go cross-country."

To his amusement, I vaulted over the fence and landed lithely on the other side. He followed, his movements fluid as always, despite his levelling up.

"The road should've gone through here," I mused as we followed the curve of the hill. "The ground is better than what we just drove through. I wonder if it was because of Camelot."

"Of course, it was. The Light and Dark here would do whatever it took to keep humans away. This place is too important."

At the top of the rise we found the first traces of the ruined castle. Stone blocks had been flung here at one point, imbedding themselves into the ground.

Grass and moss had grown over most of them, but bluestone peeked here and there through the green.

"Galahad was right," I said.

"The gift that keeps on giving," Wilder muttered.

"What? Are you jealous or something?"

He pouted and moved past me. I shook my head and laughed, following him into the darkening morning. Ahead, ruins began to emerge from the spells hiding them from the human world like shadowy spectres through a dense fog.

"This is Camelot?" Wilder asked, his bruised pride forgotten. "It's massive."

"Somehow I don't think all of it is." I stepped forwards and placed my palm against the stone. The entire vista shimmered like ripples across a still lake.

"An illusion," he murmured.

"I'd say ninety percent of this place is twisted between realities."

"Demonic and human."

I nodded. "Anything could be in there."

"It is ground zero," Wilder noted. "The portal to hell."

"You know, if this is supposed to be a pep talk, you're failing miserably."

"Look who's talking, Purples."

The castle had stretched beyond its original foundation, distorting and morphing into a nightmarish landscape. The ruins merged into passages that twisted and turned, open to the air and full of debris and gnarled vines. I could feel the power here and it wasn't all Dark. Naturals had once called this place home and their Light marked their belonging.

"I can sense the rift," Wilder said. "It's in the centre of all that."

"It's like the cataclysm tore reality apart," I mused.

"Our power did this." He breathed deeply. "Now I understand why only we can go in there."

We could decipher the illusions because the power that had been reborn into us created them.

"Then there's no time to lose." I entered the ruins, the air wavering and swallowing me whole as I stepped into the distortion.

A moment later, Wilder appeared next to me.

"I feel like I'm in *Labyrinth*," I said, looking at the numerous passages forking into various directions around us.

"Labyrinth?"

"The movie with Jennifer Connelly and David Bowie." When he shrugged, I added, "*Dance magic dance?*"

"Now you just sound crazy, Purples."

"I can't believe you've never seen *Labyrinth*!"

"I do know labyrinths are full of tricks, unforeseen dangers, and monsters…"

"Well, we have to choose a path. I don't think we can fly this time."

"The air is heavy." Wilder snorted and looked down each path. "That's a shame, flying was so much fun."

I studied the walls, wondering if there was any

hidden marks or clues. In the movie, there was an illusion hiding a secret passage. Wilder joined me, running his hands over the stonework.

"There's something here," Wilder said, waving me over. "It looks like a rune of some kind."

I stood beside him and brushed away the moss and lichen and my heart leapt. I'd recognise that rune anywhere. It was a long vertical line with four horizontal lines emerging from its right side. *Saille.* Willow.

Wilder peered at the marking. "What is it?"

"Galahad was here," I murmured.

"What do you mean?"

"This is a druidic rune. He showed this to me when we were searching for the Druids. It was on the wall of one of their caves near Bourke Castle. *Saille.* The willow tree where we found Gilhana."

Wilder's eyes widened. "He left a trail for us…"

"He risked everything to come here," I said, resting my hand against the symbol.

Returning to Camelot when it was overrun with demons was a fool's errand, but here was a symbol I recognised amongst the twisted landscape. Only Galahad could have left it, but was it before or after he'd left the note in his armour at the Academy? Eight hundred years had turned this place into a minefield, but back then… Had he made it out?

"We were never going to come here alone," I said.

"I owe that man a debt I can never repay," Wilder muttered.

"We all fight for the same cause. There is no

debt." I traced my fingers over the rune once more and took the passage it marked. "This way."

We ventured deeper into the labyrinth, the constant turns disorienting us no matter how hard we tried to keep our bearings. The stone seemed to sparkle, the broken flow of time muddying my thoughts. If it wasn't for the runes, I was sure we'd be lost in here forever.

Wilder stopped in his tracks and he grabbed my arm. "Something's coming."

"What—"

My breath caught as he pressed me against the wall. We sunk into the thick vines which seemed to conceal us from whatever threat he'd sensed. It wasn't long before I felt a familiar presence approach from the centre of the twisted reality.

The demon was just like the one I'd seen the first night I'd arrived in the past. I'd sat at Galahad's campfire as it came upon us, our only saving grace the delicate cloak the knight had placed around us. One wrong move or one minuscule sound, and we would've been dead.

The demon slunk down the passage like a slithering reptile, its black hide shimmering in the eerie light. Long arms and legs carried its elongated body as it patrolled the labyrinth, its closed mouth hiding the rows upon rows of sharpened teeth set into its massive jaw.

Wilder looked at me, his eyes asking a silent question. *Were these the demons I'd fought when I'd gone through the stones?* I nodded, and I knew he understood they still died the same way.

It passed us, neither seeing nor sensing us in the thick foliage. All seven-foot of the monster loped down the passage, its feet hardly making a sound as it traversed the crumbling maze.

I didn't know how long we waited there holding our breath as the monster turned the corner and disappeared.

"If we engage, we risk alerting them to our presence," Wilder barely whispered against my ear. "We have to go stealth on this one."

It wasn't just the noise that'd travel, any spark of Light would be detectable for miles. If we fought, we'd may as well send up a flare right now. We needed to get to the rift without being seen.

I pressed my finger to my lips and mouthed. "Quiet."

We moved out from underneath the vines and continued down the passage, finding the next rune at the end. Following it, we headed northeast.

Another demon was wandering around the corner, and we pressed our backs against the wall. I held my breath as it took a different path, narrowly missing the turn we were hiding behind. I peeked around the wall, and when I saw it was clear, I gestured for Wilder to follow.

There was no way of knowing how long we moved through the labyrinth. We were forced to hide several times as we crossed paths with the patrolling demons, but Galahad came through every time. He'd marked hidden passages and places we could catch our breath. With each one, I wished I could go back in time and thank him.

Finally, we left the labyrinth behind, emerging out into the open. The air was clear and icy and I breathed deeply, thankful to be rid of the demonic stench.

"I'm guessing this is the place," Wilder said, staring up at something.

I followed his gaze and gasped.

Camelot loomed over us, the decaying towers and parapets merely echoes of their past beauty. This place must've been something special, even for the Middle Ages.

Ahead, stairs ascended to an open courtyard, the ground covered in a layer of stone cut so precisely, the joins were barely visible. We climbed upwards, drawing our arondight hilts.

The courtyard was vast. Mosaics were laid into purposely cut depressions, the colours dulled by dirt and grit, but their scenes still as clear as the day they'd been laid. I walked over a rearing horse with a knight on its back before it joined into a larger battle scene, then a frieze of women in medieval dress using their Light with more knights surrounding them. The triple crown of the Pendragons was repeated throughout, marking the way to the great gates of Camelot.

Part of the castle had been carved into the cliff face while the rest of its walls and towers staggered down the side of the valley in an impenetrable wave. It's size was staggering—the amount of Light that must've been used to conceal this place was unfathomable. There must've been something else inside that kept human eyes away, but I wasn't sure we'd ever find it now that the Dark's claws were rent deep into the stone.

Intact, I could imagine Camelot's beauty, but even in its ruined state, it was an impressive beast. The gates were broken, the towers were torn apart, holes were gouged into the outer walls, and within, I could see the gaping tear Arthur and Lancelot had opened the night they'd crossed swords. I wondered if we could ever reclaim this place—the Naturals ancestral home—and return it to its splendour.

"C'mon," Wilder said, breaking me out of my trance, "the rift is inside."

"Wait." I grasped his wrist. "It can't be that easy. Demons were crawling through the labyrinth, but nothing stands here?"

He hesitated and looked around the open space, taking in the gates and castle walls. "You're right. They wouldn't just let us walk right in."

"We know you're there!" I shouted, my voice echoing off the rock. "Show yourself and let's get this over with!"

"*Purples!*"

"Best to flush out the rats so we can skewer them where we can see them," I told him.

Metallic footsteps echoed over the courtyard as nightmare and shadow emerged from the broken gates of Camelot. Wilder's lip curled into a snarl as

Mordred's body morphed out of the twist of Darkness.

"Did you think it would be that easy to end me?" the demon asked. "*I am eternal.*"

Man, this guy thought mighty highly of himself. He was the only one who made it super awkward. *Don't get cocky, Scarlett.*

I tightened my grip on my arondight hilt and knew he'd be more powerful here. The rift was just beyond the castle wall, feeding his mutations like a bloody solar panel. He was basically hard-wired to a never-ending battery.

His boots crunched against the debris, his cloak billowing in an unfelt breeze. "Here you are at the scene of so much suffering…the Twin Flames. You can't bring Camelot back and you can't resurrect your friends. You don't have the power. You're in our house now."

"I'm pretty sure we were here first," I drawled. "You're nothing but a stain on the carpet."

His eyes darkened, their red glow swirling into crimson. "The arrogance of your kind never ceases to amaze me."

"You were once one of us," Wilder reminded him. "Your parents—"

"I was never one of you," he snarled. "I was born into the Darkness and it has been all I've ever known. The One is my father and you invited him into your world."

I snorted. "And we've come to escort him out."

"Just like that?" Mordred swept his arm, gesturing

to the courtyard and the twisted reality around us. "Do you think it was really going to be that easy? Even now, your precious *castle* is under siege. What do you call it again…? *Castle Brent.*"

"*Lies.*" I stepped forwards and Wilder grasped my arm.

"All your modern advancements are no match for the power of the mind and spirit," Mordred went on. "The Dark may be weakened, but you make it so easy to possess your pathetic little bodies. Light is so easily *dulled.*"

"You talk a big game, Mordred," Wilder said, "but can you back it up?"

"You are all going to die," he cried. "Humanity will behold us and cower in fear. Their weapons of mass destruction will be no match for our Darkness. We will feed and consume everything in your pathetic little world until there is nothing but ash."

And then they'd find a way into the next one… and then the next, decimating everything in their path. It was their nature and their very reason for existing. They knew nothing else.

"How many?" I whispered. "How many worlds?"

Mordred fixed his burning gaze on mine. "*Countless.*"

"*And this is where it ends.*" I brought my arondight blade to life and leapt into the air, Light pushing me to dizzying heights.

I arced my blade towards his head and he twisted to the side, knocking me out of the air. I tumbled, flipping over and over before I slammed into a broken pillar. Pain erupted through my body as I landed face first on the mosaic and I gasped for breath.

"Scarlett!" Wilder roared and launched himself at Mordred.

They crossed blades, the sound of metal striking against metal ricocheting around the broken courtyard. Sparks flew, bouncing off the stone as I pushed myself to my knees. My gaze caught the mosaic underneath me, and for a split-second I saw a glimpse of Galahad. The knight below my palms was riding on a chestnut horse with his sword aloft…and etched into the stone beside it was the rune that'd led us here.

Arondight flared and I pushed to my feet with a cry, turning just as Mordred slammed Wilder into the wall beside the gate.

"It would be so easy just to let your power go," he rasped, grinding Wilder's head against the broken wall. Blood poured down his brow, over his eye, and down his cheek. "Destroy me and tear apart the way between worlds."

"It doesn't work like that, arsehole," Wilder snarled.

Mordred let out a cry of anger and threw him across the courtyard, Darkness swirling. The air began to tear apart as he summoned a slew of demonic souls like he had at the Sanctum.

I stepped forwards and Mordred turned to face me, his lip curling as he began to morph into the hulking beast of Darkness hidden within his human body.

Demons rushed towards me and I swung my blade, ducking and weaving through the storm of souls. Explosions went off in all directions as violet sparks showered the courtyard. I sensed the pull of Excalibur at the far side as Wilder worked his way towards me. Mordred was in the centre, roaring and growling as he transformed.

Suddenly, he was before me and I attacked. Darkness sparked and Mordred's blade caught mine, the shower of violet lighting up the shadows like a bolt of lightning in the centre of a terrifying storm.

I dragged the edge of my sword against his, breaking the blow, and twirled away. Dodging an Infernal, I gasped as Wilder caught it above my head, his sword slicing through it like butter. It burst into a ball of flame which was torn away by the swirling of its brethren and I was back on my feet.

Mordred lunged, his change slowing his movements, and I stabbed my sword through his right shoulder, pinning him to the wall. Wilder leapt out of the fog, his arondight blade slicing through the left.

Mordred screamed as his transformation was interrupted and began to thrash as we poured our Flame through the steel into his body.

I knew who I was. I knew who Wilder was. I knew who we were together. *I understood.*

"I don't believe in you," I snarled. "You have no power, Mordred. You only have what is given to you, and I give you *nothing.*"

"I am more powerful than you, Arondight. I have had eight lifetimes to evolve."

"It's been eight hundred years and all you've done is learn how to be an epic arsehole," I declared. "All you ever wanted was to be loved, but you were taken from your mother's arms and turned into the twisted monster before us. Darkness is all you've ever known, and we can't allow you to walk in this universe any longer."

"If you kill me, they'll all die," he cried.

"*I don't believe you.*"

"It's prophesied."

"That's the thing about prophecies, though," I drawled. "They're rarely literal, and monsters like you twist them into lies to suit your own purpose."

"I will rise again, Arondight!"

"I seriously doubt that." I slammed my hand around his neck and burst into Indigo Flame. I wasn't Arondight or Scarlett—I was pure star fire.

Wilder's hand covered mine and his Flame rushed out of him, coiling around the Light which was pulsing through me. It burned into Mordred and he screamed, his mouth gaping as liquid fire began to drip from between his lips.

The Infernals dissipated in the wind as his control waned, the wind dying completely.

"You don't know what you've done," he rasped. The liquid fire ate through his armour, his flesh burning underneath.

"It's too late for your rubbish," I hissed as we pushed one final burst of Flame into his mutated body.

Mordred screamed, the sound grating on my

bones, before he burst apart, crumbling under our touch. Our arondight blades fell to the ground with a clatter, the swords retracting into the hilts.

He was gone. Apart from the stench in the air, nothing remained of Arthur and Guinevere's only son.

"What a shame," Wilder said as he pulled his hand from mine. "To be twisted into a monster before he even drew breath…"

"What's done is done." I couldn't help but think about Jackson and the others back at Castle Brent. Had we just destroyed the hybrids? We wouldn't know until… Well, we might not ever know because there was a real chance we were going to our deaths.

I rubbed my sleeve against the blood on Wilder's forehead, but the gash was already healed.

"It's a handy trick, don't you think?" He smirked and cupped my face in his hand.

"Just don't go relying on it," I warned. "We're not immortal, Wilder."

"No, I doubt it."

I looked at the gates to Camelot and drew in a shaky breath. We hadn't even reached the rift and I was already exhausted.

"We've made it this far, Purples, no use in stopping now."

"What if he was right?" I asked. "What if the castle is being attacked? What if we just killed Jackson, Esme, Madeleine, and the others?"

"Demons lie," Wilder said. "It's their nature."

"But—"

"We can't go back." He placed his fingers on my lips. "For better or worse, we need to finish this."

I sighed and took his hand. Our Light coiled together and I tugged him towards the gate. I went through first, pulling Wilder behind me.

The courtyard extended through the gates, and I realised Camelot had been more than just a castle—it was a city. Abandoned buildings dotted the cliff side and the road leading up the incline to the main fortress. Empty windows silently judged our progress, the hairs on the back of my neck standing up.

"This is creepy," I whispered.

"We're alone," Wilder said. "We're the only ones crazy enough to come here."

"I know, it's just eerie."

We moved through a raised portcullis, passing underneath another fortified wall. This must be the inner castle where the knights and the king and queen had lived. I stepped over a shattered marble statue and rounded an empty fountain, my gaze searching the shadows, yet no threats lingered.

Nothing could come through the rift. Everything that could have had already squeezed through the night it opened.

"There." Wilder pointed and I finally saw the destruction which had torn the castle apart.

The building had been blown apart, the interior open to the elements like the back of a dollhouse. It towered over us, dark and haunting, the immense size of it breaking my heart in two.

This was the cost of merging Arondight and Excalibur with hate in our hearts—total annihilation.

We stood on the precipice of the gash and stared into the darkness. The earth had been ripped asunder like an earthquake, opening up a maw of terror. It was a blight on the beauty of Camelot, dividing the castle into two.

"Down there," Wilder said. "Can you see it?"

"It's a portal like the one I went through to get to Avalon," I told him.

"It's not the rift."

"No. It's inside."

Wilder grunted and tightened his grip on my hand. "I guess we have to jump."

I stared down into the abyss, watching the air ripple in and out of reality. Talk about a leap of faith.

"If we go through, there's no telling if we can come back out again," I said. "This could be our end."

"Then what an end it'll be."

"We didn't get to say goodbye…"

"No regrets," he told me. "They would've stopped us, but this is what we were born to do. Our path leads here and only here."

He was right. There was only the future now and it was ours to write just as Gilhana had foretold.

"I'm ready," I murmured taking his hand.

Wilder nodded and tightened his grip, then we jumped.

18

W ilder and I landed on a stone path, the sound of our boots muffled in the closeness of the changed atmosphere.

Huge blocks of stone hovered in the air held aloft by an invisible force, and the sky was tinted a burnt orange—a hue that reminded me of a Tequila Sunrise. The path continued in front of us, the smooth marble now a rough track of shiny cobblestones.

It felt as if the inside of the elaborate castle had merged with the lower section of the city which had been built up around the heart of Camelot. Time and space didn't seem to matter here, nor the laws of gravity.

Plants clung to the ruins in a strangled twist of brown and orange—no other colours seemed to thrive here—and when I looked up, chunks of earth floated like tiny islands in the sky. If I imagined hard enough, we could have been in one of Jackson's video games, VR headset and all.

"Creepy," I whispered.

It was a pocket of space and time like Avalon—a limbo between worlds.

"Our power created this," Wilder murmured.

"To think Arthur leapt into the portal and found this…" I breathed deeply and nearly gagged. It smelt like a rotten fart. "Ugh. Sulphur."

Wilder scanned the path before us. "I can see where all the association with demons and sulphur comes from."

"Great, the origin story no one asked for."

"Hold that thought, Purples." Wilder tugged on my sleeve. "We've got company, and I don't think they care about the smell."

The hairs on the back of my neck stood up as I became aware that we were being watched. As if this place couldn't get any creepier. I looked down the path and froze when I saw a dark figure in the distance.

A knight in dark grey armour stood on the path, his hands resting on a menacing-looking sword. It was the complete Medieval Knight kit—helmet, gauntlets, greaves, boots, gorget, and the other bits with their fancy names. There were even a bunch of fancy-pants feathers in his helm. He was so still, I almost believed the suit was empty, but as we moved closer, his fingers curled around the hilt.

"Halt!"

Wilder and I stopped in unison, our connection

seeming to solidify in this weird place. We were of it, yet apart.

"State your business!" the knight boomed.

"Let us pass," Wilder called out. "There's no need for us to bear arms."

The unknown knight didn't seem to like this and raised his sword, the light glinting off the sharp edge. "The way is closed."

"Then open it," I commanded. "The Twin Flames demand it." Wilder shot me a fierce look. "What? We created this place in a twisted round-about way. Claiming ownership seems like a solid plan."

"The way is *closed*," the knight shouted.

"Seems like there's only one answer," Wilder said, stating the obvious.

I was already becoming annoyed—or hangry…or the Arondight equivalent of hangry. "If the way is closed, then we'll just have to open it."

Wilder squinted at the knight. "Where's the weak spot in all that?"

"We command celestial Flame and you're asking me? Cook him in his fancy pot like the lobster he is."

As we stood bickering, the knight had closed the distance between us and swung his sword. Wilder's arondight blade sparked silver as he brought it to life. The two weapons clashed, the ring reverberating through the limbo realm.

I yelped and ducked out of the way as they clashed again and broke apart once more. Wilder struck low, the knight blocking as I circled around them, waiting for a clear shot at baking Sir Demon like a potato wrapped in aluminum foil…but he'd sensed my approach and kicked Wilder back and turned on me, his sword slashing with deadly precision.

"Scarlett! Duck!"

I gasped and fell to my knees as steel sliced just above my head. Argent Flame slammed into the knight, passing through his body, then mine, as if we weren't even there.

Arondight flared, absorbing the energy, and I brought my blade to life as the knight fell to the ground in a heap.

Wilder stood over the tangle of armour and raised his arm, his palm cracking with Argent Flame. It would be so easy for him to let it go, but he held steady.

The knight clutched his chest and dragged himself away, his armour scraping against the cobbles. "I'm free," he cried, clawing at his helm. "I'm—" He gasped as he tore the metal from his head and tossed it aside.

He was a Natural. I could see it as plain as day. His aura radiated white, pulsing with golden threads. Whatever Wilder had done had broken through the demonic possession neither of us had even sensed. Who the hell was this guy?

"It's you," Wilder rasped, lowering his arm.

"Wilder!" I cried.

He held up his hand to silence me. "He's no threat. Not anymore."

The man groaned and clutched his chest again, his armour clanking. He was obviously in a lot of pain, but I didn't think it was because of the Flame.

I looked down at the knight and studied the sharp angle of his jaw and the stubble which coated it. Messy chocolate-coloured hair was flecked with grey, and when his gaze met mine, something in his eyes felt familiar.

I stilled. The resemblance between him and Wilder… "He looks just like you."

Wilder grunted and looked over the man with a keen eye. "I think I've found my bloodline."

"Your bloodline?"

"Excalibur chose me for a reason, Purples." He gestured to the knight. "Look at him and tell me you don't recognise the king."

"The king?" I stared at the man and put two and two together. "*Arthur*."

Wilder stared down at him. "Excalibur was broken and its power was lost."

"But it wasn't," I argued. "You're right here. It had to go somewhere."

"It did," he said. "It was just waiting for the right time to reveal itself."

"It was waiting for Arondight to return," Arthur whispered. "Without me, it would've passed to my son, but he was taken from us."

"Gwain," I said. "He carried on the Pendragon bloodline."

Arthur's family had lived on, ensuring Excalibur had something to come back to if it was found. What they understood of the sword or if they were a part of the Order of the Twin Flames was unknown, but here we were.

"It doesn't matter," Wilder said. "I don't know who my parents were and knowing this doesn't shed any light on who they might've been. I'm Excalibur, and that's all I need to know."

"You know your legacy," I said, "your history. It's a start, isn't it?"

"Perhaps. If we're able to return."

Arthur pushed himself into a seated position and leaned against the wall. His eyes looked sunken and I got the feeling he was aging right before our eyes. Whatever had controlled him had likely stopped him from withering away. Now that it was gone, time and nature were catching up with him. If we had questions, now was the time to ask them.

I knelt beside the once king and helped him take off his gauntlets. The cold iron clattered onto the cobblestones and he let out a heaving sigh.

"What happened to you?" I asked.

"My jealousy tore our world apart. I did what I had vowed not to. I used Excalibur with a tainted heart and how many died for it? Too many to count…"

"What's done is done," I told him.

"Lancelot," he said, grasping my arm. "What happened to him?"

"You don't want to ask about your wife?" Wilder asked with a scowl.

"I know what happened to her," Arthur

murmured. "They took Guinevere and our unborn child… They tormented me with her screams. They left me here, possessed and in chains, guarding their putrid abyss."

"*Wilder*," I hissed. I then turned to Arthur. "Lancelot went looking for atonement. He searched for Guinevere and penance."

"He survived?"

I nodded slowly. "For a time. The knights of Camelot found him a few years after, but he was already gone and Arondight was missing. He was buried in Avalon beside you as you both wished."

"Merlin," the king said with a sad smile.

"It seems so. The Druids hid Lancelot's sword in time until its power was reborn. Merlin was there until the end, but they've gone now."

"To their homeland." Arthur coughed, his chest heaving with the effort. "The old man always threatened to leave us when I wouldn't listen."

I smiled softly. "Sounds like something a Druid would do."

I knew Arthur had a lot of questions, so I did my best to tell him what I could. I told him how the knights of Camelot rebuilt in the years after the cataclysm. How we'd expanded all over the world, our Academy, our beliefs, and how Percival created the Codex. We'd become strong again, but now we were at the brink. The final battle was already under way.

I held Arthur's hands. "We're here to put an end to it."

"Then perhaps you can do what I could not." He

coughed again and wiped his mouth, the back of his hand smeared with blood. "I don't deserve forgiveness, only the justice you are owed."

"What?" I asked. "What do you mean?"

Wilder knelt on the other side of Arthur. "He means to die, Purples."

"But he's already dying," I hissed.

He looked at the king. "Not like that."

"This calamity is my doing," Arthur said. "I vowed to bring peace to our world, but instead, I tore it apart. I submit to your sword, Excalibur, and accept my punishment willingly."

He wanted Wilder to execute him? I looked between them and tears began to well in my eyes. This was to be the end of the great Arthur Pendragon?

With wild eyes, Arthur grasped Wilder's shirt. "Excalibur, they can enter from their world, but they cannot pass into ours."

"I understand."

The One. My heart began to thrum painfully as I realised we were in deep shite. I knew closing the rift wasn't going to be easy, but at least we were on an even playing field. That was something, right?

"He will come before the end," Arthur said. "*He will come*."

"We'll be ready," Wilder murmured, pressing his palm over the old king's heart. "The Twin Flames will triumph."

Arthur's lips curved into a serene smile. "*For the Light*."

"For the Light."

Silver flame began to glow from Wilder's right palm and Arthur gasped, grabbing for his left. "*Remember.*"

The flame grew, Light streaming from underneath the king's armour. Finally, it enveloped his entire body and he crumbled from within, turning to ash before my eyes.

I choked back a sob as I lowered my gaze, saying a final prayer as Arthur Pendragon took his last breath.

Ash fell through Wilder's fingers and he blinked away his tears. He was hurting, knowing his legacy had been so intimately tied to the destruction our world faced. It wasn't just Excalibur, but the part of his soul that was Natural, too.

It wasn't the same for me—I was just a random chosen to become Arondight—but it didn't mean I couldn't feel it. Arthur was the hero of all the stories, but at the end… He'd done what he could, just the same as all of us.

Wilder rose to his feet, staring at something on his palm. Turning, he showed me what Arthur had given him in his last moments.

It was a cold iron signet ring, the crest emblazoned with the three Pendragon crowns, encrusted with yellow gemstones and diamonds. I reached out and closed his fingers around the treasure —it was precious, just like him.

"He chose his end," I murmured. "He's with the Light now. His soul is free from the Dark, thanks to you."

"Wilder Pendragon doesn't have a good ring to it," he muttered.

"We can always call you Wilbur." He stared at me and I added, "It's Wilder and Excalibur joined together."

"I would laugh, but…" He looked down at the remains of Arthur, his great-great-great—I didn't know how many greats—whatever he was. "Everything makes sense at the end. All the loose threads are tying up."

I turned to the path where at the end, the way between limbo and hell awaited. "All but one."

"Acceptance is a strange thing," he muttered. "I thought it would take time, but seeing his life burn away… He was my only surviving family."

"We can't know that for sure."

Wilder laughed, not in amusement but in resignation. "I have a knowing about it, Purples. I feel it's true, just can't explain why."

There were words to say at a time like this but I couldn't think of what they were, so I told him, "I wish I knew what to say."

"Maybe there aren't any words." He looked towards the portal. "We can't wait any longer. I can feel the Darkness building."

Wilder slipped the ring into his pocket and put his arondight blade away, and together, we walked along the path where a platform rose at the end. There was nothing else we could do, there was no going back.

"Arthur wasn't just a guardian," I said, piecing my

thoughts together, "he was a conduit. It's how the One was able to control Brax."

"A bridge between worlds."

"And now we've severed it."

"Tripped the alarm," Wilder added with a finality that was chilling.

I stepped up onto the platform and swept my hand through the air. The portal rippled, revealing itself to us. Wilder stood beside me, his presence comforting as we gathered the courage to fulfil our destiny. We'd merge and it would either be the beginning or the end. The fate of our world would be decided here.

Wilder took my hand and together, we looked through the tear into an alien world.

19

———

W e stood on the brink of desolation and our souls screamed into the Darkness.

The Dark's world had been someone else's and now it was black, the atmosphere stripped to a mere whisper…just enough for the demons to cling to its surface and wait for the rift to open.

How could anything make it out of this horror? They stripped everything away until nothing—not plants, animals, intelligent life-forms—had any hope of survival. If this was an alternate Earth, and Wilder and I failed, then our future was bleak indeed.

There was an unbearable weight pressing against my chest. "We can't just close the rift and leave others to this fate. I can't—"

"Countless," Wilder murmured. "Mordred said they'd done this to countless worlds. I can't even imagine how many lives have been stripped from existence."

"We have to stop him," I said.

"He's coming."

I nodded. I could feel the approaching storm, the stars of a different world shining down on us through the tear.

"He's the most powerful demon of them all," Wilder reminded me. "We know nothing about him. He could be immortal. He could have millennia of power stored inside him. He could wipe us out with a flick of his wrist."

"He could be a lot of things, but I fought him at the Academy."

"He was in Brax's body and severely weakened."

"And he won't let us die. He needs us to open the rift." I took his hands in mine. "We know what it's going to take to close it, but the One doesn't. If we fail, he'll force us to merge and he'll get a rude shock."

"We can trap him in here." *With us to keep him company…* It all seemed like a small price to pay.

"*Yes.*"

"If we fight him here, we can cut him off from the other demons," Wilder said.

"He'd be one step away from our world…"

"I know, but it's an even playing field. We let him in, close the rift—"

"And blow this pocket of space and time into oblivion."

"Purples…" he took a deep breath, "we might not walk away from this. We can save our world and return home, but we have to do it now. If we try to save infinite worlds—"

"I know," I whispered. "But he could follow the Druids through the Darklands. Or he could find a way into another reality where they don't have anyone to fight for them. He could consume alternative versions of our friends. And then he could find another way into our world. We have the power to stop him for good. What are our lives compared to an unfathomable amount of others?"

"Damn your conscious," he said.

"Doing the right thing is hard, but I can't walk away. And I know you can't, either."

"No," he shook his head, looking to the rift, "I can't, but you already knew that. When we merged, everything was on show, Purples."

"There's a dirty joke in that."

Wilder grasped my hand and I heard his heartbeat skip. "He's here."

We had to wait until he was in the limbo-verse. The One was like cancer, if even a part of him remained behind there was a possibility he could regenerate. We'd seen demons do it before and this was the greatest there ever was. Nothing was off the table where this arsehole was concerned.

Darkness ebbed through the rift, pushing through the tear, and I held onto Wilder's hand, his touch grounding me and silencing my rising fear.

The One was an immense shadow figure like something out of a paranormal ghost hunting show. Black limbs oozed out of the portal and spilled onto the ground as he pried himself through the widening gap.

Without a body to channel his essence through, he was unable to speak, but my head began to throb the moment he looked down upon us.

I am the One. His voice was molten iron in my mind as he moved towards us, his entire form now in the limbo realm. *I am the pinnacle. I am death, destruction, and pain.*

I'd heard those words before. He'd spoken them to me through Brax when we stood outside the Academy. However, they were even more ominous now that we were looking upon the One's true form.

I am here to take your world. Open the rift and let the horde pass. You have no power over my true form, Twin Flames. You have failed.

"Like hell," I snarled. "We're here to make sure you never take another world."

Pain twisted through my head and I fell to my knees, gasping. Wilder drew his arondight blade and snarled.

Your world is rich with souls, the One projected. *Souls that fight.*

"You'll never have it," Wilder exclaimed. "We won't allow it."

I've fought your kind before, Celestial. You are nothing against the Dark.

The shadow wrapped itself around Wilder and he was flung through the air, first one way, then jerked violently back to the other. His head snapped to the side and his limbs flailed, the force too much for him to fight against. His arondight blade clattered to the ground, useless.

Gashes began to open over his body, cut by an unseen force. I screamed as blood poured from him and my arondight blade sparked violet. I slashed through the shadows, but the sword passed without leaving any mark. Desperate to free Wilder, I called upon my Flame and leapt towards him with my arms outstretched.

We collided and I held onto him as we fell out of the inky darkness and plummeted through the air. We landed in a heap, my body taking the brunt of the impact.

I gasped as Wilder rolled to the side and winced in pain. Connected to the horde on the other side of the rift, the One was too powerful. He'd just swept into the limbo realm and tore us apart like we were nothing. We hadn't even had a chance to land a single blow. He'd steamrolled us and we never saw it coming.

Suddenly, I understood how they were able to take so many worlds against a force like ours. How were we going to stand against him where so many failed?

The One let out a guttural growl, his shadowy head turning towards us. *Die,* he projected into our minds. *Die and let your hate bloom…*

Wilder shuddered, his control over Excalibur fading as mine was slipping into dangerous territory. The One knew I was the weak link—he'd been living amongst us for years and had been there the day I'd first arrived at the Sanctum. He understood who we were and how we thought.

He'd attacked Wilder, knowing I'd never be able

to live without him. He knew if he was dead, I'd turn on him in hate…and then it'd all be over.

"Don't listen to him," I cried, fisting my hands into Wilder's blood-soaked shirt. "This is what he wants."

Arondight flared, calling for Excalibur to rise, but I shoved it down. My hold was tenuous at best, the looming presence of the One piercing my mind.

Hate would be our undoing.

The rift was opening, the way between our worlds almost wide enough for the One to step through and begin his campaign of terror.

I curled over Wilder's broken body and held him close, unable to stop my tears.

"I love you," he rasped. "I just wish I'd said it more…"

"Shut up," I murmured. "It's not over yet, you know."

"Scarlett… I'm dying. Without—"

I pressed my lips to his and kissed him softly, ignoring the tang of blood on his tongue. "You don't get to say shite like that, you hear me? We're here, we love one another, and we have nothing left to lose. While that idiot salivates over his false positive, we merge. *One last time*."

"Purples…"

I brushed my fingers over his lips. "If you go, I go with you. That's how it will always be."

His eyes were glassy, and I could feel him slipping away, but he nodded. "One last time."

In that moment knowing was all we had. We knew what we had to do, we understood what we faced.

We'd looked into the abyss and saw his true nature. Now we fought for *all* worlds.

The One was a hive mind, connected to the horde beyond. Once he was gone, the rest would fall, but those on Earth were already on their own. All worlds would be safe from utter destruction, but not from danger. No one was absolute, not even us.

Arondight wrapped around Excalibur and our Light pulsed. The sound of the One's roar of triumph tested our faith, but our love was strong as we ignited. We rose as one and the limbo realm began to shudder and quake, blocks of stone falling from the sky as reality disintegrated around us.

Wilder and I were pure flame, twisting around one another, burning brightly and without end.

Love held us together as we collided with the One, lighting the shadow from within. We reached out, clawing at the edges of the limbo realm and pulled them towards us, wrapping ourselves in the essence of the universe. It was a blanket of starlight, comforting and full of promise.

The One screamed in our minds, thrashing and fighting against the pressure bearing down on him.

One last time, Excalibur said to Arondight before he kissed her.

Time and space slammed shut, swallowing the Darkness whole, and the Twin Flames plummeted back to…back to where?

The light faded and darkness was all they knew.

20

"**S**carlett!"

My eyes cracked open, revealing darkness all around. I felt heavy as a lump of lead sinking to the bottom of the ocean. Down, *down…*

"Scarlett! *Wilder!*"

Above, the sky was grey with splashes of blue. *Earth.*

I breathed in the cool air and coughed as my throat scratched. Rolling over, I grimaced as my limbs throbbed and stung. Wilder lay beside me, but he wasn't moving.

"Wilder," I rasped, tugging his shirt. It was stiff with blood and dirt.

We were lying in the centre of a crater as if we'd slammed into the Earth like a flaming meteorite. After all the things we'd done, I wouldn't be surprised if that's exactly what'd happened when the limbo-verse imploded on us and the One.

I dragged myself over Wilder and pressed my ear against his chest. *Please be beating. Please, please, please…*

A soft *ba-boom, ba-boom* thrummed inside him and I began to cry. Clutching his shirt, I sobbed as his flame began to stir.

I was so relieved, I didn't realise when rocks bounced down the side of the crater until a shadow loomed over us. Turning, I shielded Wilder with my body and raised my hand.

"Scarlett!"

I blinked, my breath catching and I let my power go. "Jackson?"

He waved with both hands over his head, calling out to someone in the distance. "Over here! They're over here!" Then he skidded down the side of the depression, landing next to us with all the grace of an elephant with two left feet.

I pushed off the ground and threw my arms around him with a relieved cry. We were like two chalkboard dusters clapping together and dust and debris showered everywhere.

"Thank God you're okay," he cried, his voice muffled in my hair.

"When we killed Mordred, I thought… He said—" I grasped his arms and stared at my best friend, giving him a little shake to make sure he was real. The little red lightning bolts that'd sparked amongst his aura were gone… "*Jackson.*" I looked over him and grasped his face, staring into his eyes. "What happened to you?"

He laughed, tears filling his eyes. "I'm human,

Scarlett. I don't know what you did, but…we're human. All of us."

I gasped, unable to speak. I looked at Wilder, but he was still unconscious.

"Is he okay?" Jackson asked, moving to check his pulse.

"He was hurt pretty bad, but I think he's going to be okay." I swallowed and gazed up at the sky. "Where are we?"

"Camelot," he said, "well, what's left of it."

"How?"

"We came looking for you as soon as we—"

A loud curse echoed above us as Aldrich looked down over the crater with us inside. He scratched his head, then clambered down the side of the crater to join us.

"Never in my life…" he said, helping me to sit.

"The castle?" I asked, tugging at his sleeve. "Please tell me the others are okay."

"They came out of nowhere," he told me, confirming what Mordred had taunted us with. "Infected and possessed. They assaulted the castle and we had no choice but to fight."

"Not long after, they just dropped," Jackson added. "They fell over like dominoes."

My heart leapt into my throat. "Did they die?"

Aldrich shook his head. "They were freed, Scarlett. Whatever you and Wilder did, it saved them. That's how we knew you succeeded."

I nodded. "It's done. We're free."

"Thank the Light. Can you walk?" I nodded and

he gestured to Jackson. "Give me a hand with Wilder."

I pushed to my knees, wincing as a sharp pain stabbed through my ribs. "Where are we going?"

"The Academy," Aldrich replied. "Castle Brent was nice, but it was too drafty."

"He's such an old man," Wilder rasped.

I cried out and turned to find him propped up on his elbows. His gaze met mine and I was never so glad to be alive as that moment.

"I know, I know," he drawled. "I live to die another day."

I sat on the bench beside the Thames, watching as a crane lifted a heavy load onto a building site in Battersea.

The Sanctum was being rebuilt, and all around the world there were others just like it being repaired and fortified. The weather had held off enough to get the building started, and it was a mild winter this year. Since the ground hadn't frozen, the foundations were going in without a hitch, though it helped when there was a little Light involved.

New life was blossoming out of the ashes of our near-miss and it was glorious.

After a month recovering at the Academy in the Cotswolds—featuring a lively Christmas—it was kind of nice to be back in the city. Wilder had spent his time learning how to fly, which was annoying because

I never knew which direction he was coming from, but it took his love of heights to a whole new level. He was happy, and in turn, it made me happy.

Our presence had been a bit of a disruption for the students—all they wanted to do was hang out with us and forget about their studies, much to Islington's annoyance—so we'd returned to London with Greer and Aldrich to help them take out the trash before the builders could get into the Sanctum.

"It's a refreshing way to bring in the new year, don't you think?"

I looked up to see Greer approach across the grass. She was huddled in a black woollen coat with a cream scarf bundled around her neck.

She'd been busy, too. Not only was she and Aldrich overseeing the rebuilding of the Sanctum, but she was busy adding new pages into the Codex. Wilder and I had been helping, and Aiden, of course—he'd never forgive us if he couldn't help record the tale. We had a few loose threads of our own to add to the history of the Naturals, and I think Greer was relieved for his help in the end.

All of it was so overwhelming—my journey back in time, our awakenings, Camelot and the fate of Arthur Pendragon, our stand-off with the One, and the closing of the rift. Not to mention the rest of it…

"I don't know where you get the money," I said. "Wherever it is, it seems to be a bottomless pit I'd like to dive into."

Greer laughed. "You're looking at hundreds of years of good investing."

"That's a damn fine financial planner. If you've got their card, I'll take it."

She sat beside me and we watched the crane lower an impressive steel beam into the centre of the building site. So much history had been destroyed, but we'd do whatever it took to make sure it was never forgotten again.

"What now?" I asked, listening the sounds of the city. "I hate being idle…makes my feet itchy."

"The war is over, but there's still plenty of work to be done. Demons are still here, and they'll be dealt with. Aldrich is coordinating with the other survivors as they rebuild. New York and Los Angeles are already discussing strategies."

"When all the demons have been rounded up, what do you think we'll do?"

"What we were supposed to do," she replied simply. "The Naturals existed a thousand years before the cataclysm—a fact we know thanks to you—and there were no demons then. We shall protect the Earth and her people. What that means, I don't know yet."

"But you will," I told her. "If anyone knows what's good for us, it's you, Greer."

She grinned and looked back to the Sanctum. "It warms my heart knowing we can finally stand here and be friends, Scarlett. What you and Wilder did for this world—"

"Was nothing."

"No." Greer shook her head. "It was *everything*."

A gust of air buffeted us and I turned to see

Wilder. He'd landed on the grass and was grinning from ear to ear. He'd become even more of a self-involved smart-arse now that he was supercharged, but I had to admit I got lost in it sometimes, too.

"I'm really getting the hang of the landing," he said, his lips quirking.

I rolled my eyes. "Smug arsehole."

"I have to get back," Greer said, checking her watch. "Aldrich is waiting for me."

"Can I give you a lift?" Wilder asked.

She paled slightly and shook her head. "Uh, no thank you. I prefer getting around the old-fashioned way."

Wilder sat beside me as Greer made her hasty retreat. I wasn't sure if she declined because she was afraid of heights or his loose grip.

"Hey, did you hear the good news?" I asked, bumping my shoulder against his.

He slapped a kiss on top of my head. "What good news?"

"Jackson proposed to Esme."

Wilder raised his eyebrows. "It's a wonder Greer hasn't offered to officiate the proceedings."

"She already has," I said with a smirk. "I never knew there was a Natural wedding ceremony."

"Don't look at me like that. I'm not marriage material."

"If we weren't mystical alien-hybrids, I would dump you for that comment."

"Lucky for me we transcend human ceremonies," he said with a wicked grin.

I grasped his chin and shook his head and he swatted me away with a laugh.

Jackson and Esme may be human again, but it didn't mean they'd lost their place at the Sanctum. The remaining forces of the Dark would try to cling on as hard as they could, and that meant they'd do just about anything to survive. Human Convergence could be brought back with a vengeance, or any number of diabolical plans to undermine our authority. Their help would be welcome, and they were honorary Naturals these days.

The best part about curing everyone of their demon mutations was seeing Madeleine return to the Academy with her Light intact—it was the ultimate cherry on the cake. She'd graduate in the summer and become a full-fledged Natural and join the fight —just as she'd always dreamed—and her family would be there to see it happen.

So many had been lost when Mordred had risen —families had been broken apart and souls had been lost. Hunter's family in New York had been taken from him, Alo had lost Valeria, the love of his life, and Romy had suffered the death of Martin—but we still had their memory, just like I had of Galahad, Bedivere, the knights of Camelot, and Gilhana. Every single soul who had appeared on the path to this moment would never be forgotten.

"Aiden said he was trying to convince the Regula to let him lead an archeological expedition to Camelot," Wilder said.

"Since when?"

"Since I just saw him at the Sanctum."

I grunted, wondering if Aiden would ask us to go along on his archeological dig. "Wow, the Regula's back, huh?"

"We need someone to bring us all together. Arthur did it once, and we need to be united now more than ever."

"Who volunteered as tribute?" I drawled.

He coughed nervously.

I gasped. "*You didn't…*"

"I'm still recovering from my concussion," he declared. "And I'm the man who signs the permission slips. If you want something, now's the perfect time to ask."

I took Wilder's hand and studied the Pendragon ring on his thumb. I was glad he'd decided to wear it and declare for his family. He was basically royalty in a weird way, but thankfully, we'd done without a monarchy for a few centuries now.

"It's ironic, isn't it?" Wilder asked, watching me twist the ring around his thumb. "All my life I rebelled against authority, only to find out I'm a bloody Pendragon."

"Don't let it go to your head."

He snorted and wrapped his free arm around me. "I never got the chance to thank you properly."

I looked up at him and frowned. "For what?"

"For saving my life."

"It was a fluke. I had no idea merging would bring you back like it did. I was prepared to go down in flames beside you, so to speak."

He smiled and pressed his forehead against mine. "No, not for that."

I made a face. "You're high. What else could it be?"

"The night you followed the illusion I'd put on the troll doll, I was one heartbeat away from being exiled."

My breath caught. "I never knew that."

"I was wondering what the point of fighting was," he went on, his voice lowering. "I was tossing up whether to go rogue or just end it all."

I tensed. "*Wilder*."

"But you walked in and were an utter raging bitch."

"*Excuse me*." I slapped him on the arm.

He laughed and reached into his jacket and pulled out a troll doll, just like the one I'd lost in the Sanctum. "I promised I'd get you a new one, but I couldn't find any," he told me. "So, I found the old one in the rubble and gave it a wash. I hope you like vintage."

I snatched the ugly plastic toy from his hands and threw my arms around Wilder's neck, holding both of them as tightly as I could. Who knew I'd feel so strongly about my troll lookalike?

He breathed deeply, returning my embrace. "I'm sorry I couldn't find Galahad's letter or your mother's arondight blade."

"It's okay. The universe is safe, that's all that matters."

"And you," he added.

We sat together, watching the building site, the troll doll sitting in my lap. It would be months before the Sanctum would be complete. Until then, the UK base of operations would remain at the Academy.

"What now?" I asked. "Do you have to fly off on a promotional tour with the Regula?"

He snorted. "Don't you have to go help Esme shop for a wedding dress or something?"

I groaned. "Don't remind me. I know nothing about that stuff. I was mainly referring to all that." I gestured to the building site. "You know, the bit that comes after saving the world. All the stories end before they get to that part."

"Well, first things first," Wilder grinned and looked out over London, "we've got some mopping up to do."

"Kicking demonic arse? Talk about an epic date night. *Oh, Wilbur.*"

Wilder took my hand and his eyes flashed silver. "Let's fly."

Arondight flared and together, we took flight, leaving London far below with nothing but stars above.

The End...

Thank you for reading the Arondight Codex! I hope you have enjoyed it as much as I did writing it.

Stay tuned for THE CAMELOT ARCHIVE, a new series starring Madeleine, coming in 2020!

If you would like to be notified when the first book is released, please sign up for my mailing list at:

nicolertaylorwrites.com/newsletter

Keep reading for an exclusive sneak peek...

ABOUT NICOLE

Nicole R. Taylor is an Australian Urban Fantasy author.

She lives in the western suburbs of Melbourne dreaming up nail biting stories featuring sassy witches, duplicitous vampires, hunky shapeshifters, and devious monsters.

She likes chocolate, cat memes, and video games.

When she's not writing, she likes to think of what she's writing next.

Follow Nicole Online:

Website: www.nicolertaylorwrites.com
Twitter: twitter.com/nicole_noir
Facebook: facebook.com/nrtaylorwrites
Newsletter: www.nicolertaylorwrites.com/newsletter
Email: nicole.this.is@gmail.com

DEMON BOUND (THE CAMELOT ARCHIVE - BOOK ONE)

Madeleine Greenbriar, what have you gotten yourself into this time?

The lingering scent of sulphur tickled my nostrils as I walked down the dark street, the trail leading me towards Islington High Street.

Dammit, it was trying to hide.

I could hear the throb of heavy music before I turned the corner and my heart sank and rose, if such a thing was possible.

The line for the nightclub snaked down the block, humans dressed in their best outfits. Death-rockers, punks, and goths huddled in their cliques as they waited to get inside London's longest running alternative venue, *Adrenaline.*

Mohawks, tattoos, and piercings were the flavour of the subculture, along with corsets, buckles, and elaborate hair extensions. There were a few futuristic looks—android-esque with plastic tubing hair and spiked welding goggles—and others wore more traditional goth attire made up of lace and velvet… and then there was me.

I had the all black thing down pat, but my profession demanded I paired the colour with tactical gear. Trousers with pockets, an arondight blade—a magical blade that retracted into its hilt—at my left hip, a cold iron dagger made from a meteorite on my right, and another in my combat boot. The rest of the uniform was a simple tight black T-shirt and a leather jacket. The last bit was an amendment on my part. My last shred off rebelliousness now that I was a full-fledged Natural warrior. At least my hair was naturally dark.

I scanned the crowd, my senses coming up blank. My target wasn't out here.

I walked past the line of humans, my boots thudding against the uneven concrete. The security guards checking ID didn't bother to lift their heads as I passed, but they wouldn't have seen me even if they did. The first rule of patrolling was to remain concealed at all times.

I was a Natural—a demon-hunting mage—born to fight the Darkness from beyond the rift. Even though the rift was closed five years ago, it didn't mean we ridded the world of the demons who sought to consume it. We'd gone from soldiers in a war to the cleanup crew. It wasn't the kind of hero I wanted to be, but after I'd almost become a casualty of said war before I'd even graduated from the Academy, I supposed manning a mop wasn't all that bad.

That's how I found myself on the hunt at a goth

club, of all places. I wasn't supposed to be patrolling solo, but I'd ditched my partner hours ago, frustrated by the rules and regulations—and the distrustful glances she kept throwing at me. It was a recurring routine that pissed me off more than I should've allowed.

I worked better alone.

Inside, the venue was nothing more than a rundown warehouse of patched concrete. Four levels rose above me like a maze, full of clubbers and Light knew what else. Music vibrated through the structure, feeding into my heightened senses. I'd always wanted time off to go clubbing at the city's premier alternative club, but there was never any rest for a Natural. This was as good as it was going to get.

Adrenaline was a place outsiders could come and express themselves without fear of being ridiculed, which was an admirable feat, but no one ever stopped to think about how the outsiders judged their own just as harshly. It was a human failing, despite striving for acceptance beyond the norm.

Then there was the other drawback of being different. Goths—more than any other human subculture—dabbled in demonic summoning the most. I didn't know why humans would want to mess with the Dark, but I knew there were humans out there who thrived on shock value. Wearing a corset as an outer layer, shaving half your hair off and colouring it black and blue, wasn't enough for some people.

Following the blip on my Light radar, I moved

through the club, rising through the heaving mass of bodies. I passed a room playing traditional goth music and narrowed my eyes at the humans twisting their hands towards the ceiling, their long, lace sleeves trailing through the mist from a smoke machine. It was a dance dubbed 'cobwebs in the ceiling'.

Snorting, I passed the door and kept climbing. It wasn't until I reached the top that I stopped. The stench of demonic activity was potent—the putrid fart smell curling my nose. It was no wonder no one else seemed to notice it. The club was a melting pot of scents—stale beer, sweat, urinal cakes, the sickly aroma from the smoke machine, and the damp that always clung to old buildings like this one. No amount of pine disinfectant could cover all of that.

The bass of a heavy industrial song reverberated through the concrete floor, pulsing up my legs and into my body. The flashing lights cast an eerie glow over the goths dancing around me, their movements stuttering like an elaborate stop-motion animation.

It wasn't hard to spot my target. It had leeched its Darkness all over the club like a putrid snail trail.

I watched the demon slide up against a woman in a sleek, black PVC corset. It'd inhabited a man's body or had taken on the appearance of one. I wouldn't know until I got closer.

It seemed the rarer cast of demons had fallen out of the woodwork since the rift had closed. The lesser, more rotting kind had fallen apart in the last few years and the big boys had come out to play in their frantic search for power. It meant demon hunting had become a wild new frontier.

They began to dance together, her hands snaking around his neck. *If only she knew.*

But I did, and it made watching its seduction even creeper knowing it was after her soul.

That's when I realised it'd screwed me over.

The club was a tight space, every inch used to its full capacity. That meant there were no dark corners or storage closets to drag my prey inside. I couldn't draw my arondight blade without hurting an innocent, and I couldn't do an exorcism because its putrid demonic arse would just fly off into someone else. And then I'd have to repeat the whole ordeal over again…and I loathed repeating myself.

It was a fight that might end badly, no matter what I did. I risked exposure of our kind by confronting it here, or the soul of an innocent if I choose to stand down.

I sighed. I couldn't walk away knowing I would damn her soul to complete erasure, despite her crimes to fashion.

The only way to end this was to wrestle the demon outside.

I slid through the crowd, silent and invisible, flowing past flailing arms and stomping boots, my form melting through the flashing lights. The demon didn't notice me until I was upon them.

I pressed my hand on the woman's shoulder, sending a flutter of Light—the magic that set me apart from humanity—into her. She blinked, then moved away from the threat, her gaze passing straight through the man she'd just been rubbing up against as if he'd never been there.

Once she was gone, I pulled the demon into the aura of my cloak, concealing it from the surrounding humans.

"Natural," it hissed.

"No soul eating for you tonight," I declared, closing my hand around its throat. "How about you and I take this outside?"

"Stupid girl. You're going to die."

It lunged, sending me flying back into the wall of dancers. The crowd parted, clubbers looking around to see what had pushed them out of the way.

I landed flat on my back with the creature on top of me, its hands clawing at my neck.

The moment skin touched skin, I could sense what it was. It wasn't an Infernal—a cloudy essence possessing a human—it was something else. Something new. It was evolving to survive in a world cut off from its power source. We'd been warned about this.

Its tongue grew, as did the barbs along it, and licked towards my face. I pushed my Light into it, my free hand scrambling for my arondight blade. The creature screeched as my power burned its flesh.

Our desperate struggle was cut short as the demon burst into a fireball above me. Gasping, I covered my face with my arm as heat blasted my exposed skin.

My Light went into overdrive. I pushed off the

floor, flipping to my feet. My hand closed around my sword hilt as I looked for my rescuer…or assailant—I wasn't quite sure what I'd just walked into.

An ebb of unknown power drew my attention to a man lingering in the shadows and our gazes met.

Tall, dark, and handsome had nothing on this guy. Sharp, angled jaw, piercing eyes, shaved head, lean muscle, dressed in black…but he wasn't a clubber. He wore jeans that were torn at the knees, battered combat boots, a tight, washed-out T-shirt, and a leather biker jacket that had seen better days. Rugged and dangerous—just how I liked my men, which made him a threat.

He lifted his finger to his lips, his eyes flashed silver as the strobe light pulsed above us.

I froze, my Light sensing the Darkness lingering just below the surface of his human exterior. It was also in that moment that I realised my cloak had failed and the entire fourth floor of *Adrenaline* was staring at me.

The man smirked and melted into the gap between a girl with a massive teased mohawk and a guy in black PVC pants and matching waist cincher.

I lunged after him, pushing through the humans. They shouted at me over the pounding music, but I wasn't focused on them. A flash of tired black leather led me out the door and down the stairs. Barrelling past a swarm of startled goths, I chased my newest target through the club, ducking under outstretched arms and twisting around stomping cyber goths on yet another dance floor.

A demon killing one of its own kind? Stranger things had happened, but they rarely went down like this. I got the feeling the newcomer was helping me out, but I'd learned from an early age not to have such high hopes in people, demonic or otherwise.

I could be running into another trap, but this was too strange not to follow up.

Just as security rushed into the venue, I made it outside where I was invisible again.

I legged it down the lane, my Light propelling me over the slick cobblestones, and veered around the corner. Following the whiff of Dark, I turned left in time to catch sight of my target ducking into another lane ahead.

Chasing him, I skidded around the building. Leaping into the air, I propelled myself over the row of parked motorcycled and mopeds, grazed a spiked fence, and landed in the terrace gardens. They were locked green spaces for the private use of the people living in the posh houses either side, but tonight they were just yet another obstacle in a chase scene.

I paid no attention to the night around me as I sprinted down the path, following the demon. Ahead, he jumped into a tree, then swung from a light pole.

Preempting his next move, I sprang over the fence and pushed off the ground with a burst of Light. I flew through the air and drew my arondight blade. Landing on the roof of the terrace, my boots clattered against the old terracotta tiles.

I was in the man's path.

I swung my sword, the blade erupting out of the

hilt. Silver shards of Light sparked as it slammed into the brick chimney stack centimetres from his face. He'd barely come to a halt in time, but luckily for him, we both had a second sight for these kinds of situations.

"I'd be careful with that thing," he said. "You could take someone's eye out."

They were the first words he had spoken, and his accent threw me. It was Scottish, but it wasn't. Another twang hid in there, though I couldn't figure it out.

"Give me one good reason why I shouldn't send you back to Hell," I demanded.

"Only one? I can give you a thousand." He smirked.

He began to move, and I forced my blade towards his face, but he ducked, avoiding the blow too fast for my liking. I pirouetted, arcing a full three-sixty degrees, only to slam my sword on the other side of the chimney stack, blocking his path again.

"Okay, okay," he said, holding up his hands as silver sparks danced across the roof.

"Start. *Talking.*"

"I've got no fight with you, Natural, but I can't be caught here."

I narrowed my eyes, my gaze piercing his Darkness. That's when I saw it—something I recognised from a long time ago. I knew what to look for, because I'd had the same thing growing inside me —a mutation. "You're not entirely Dark."

He smirked. "Takes one to know one."

I hesitated, and that split-second gave him an opening to strike.

He pushed me backwards with a pulse of Darkness and wrenched my blade from my hand. My boot slipped on the tiled roof and I was falling.

Air rushed past me and I let go of my Light, the burst of energy softening the blow as I landed flat on my back in the garden. My sword speared the ground next to my head, the blade imbedding so close, I felt the breeze flutter against my cheek. My heart leapt into my throat and I pushed to my feet, cursing.

Son of a…

I wrenched my arondight blade free and took off after the man. I was not letting him get away.

Human Convergence was dead. It'd ended forever the night the rift had closed. Scarlett and Wilder—the Twin Flames—had killed Mordred, the source of all demonic mutations, and we'd been cured. *We'd been cured.*

I jumped off the end of the row of terrace houses and landed on the footpath of Islington High Street. I stood on the corner, watching as a red double-decker bus zoomed past, and threw my hands into the air.

The man was gone.

***

Continue the adventure in:
THE CAMELOT ARCHIVE

Demons, Druids, and buried secrets. The Camelot Archive is open for business.

Demon Bound #1
Demon Sworn #2
Demon Forged #3
Demon Eternal #4

Druids, witches, fae, and shapeshifters abound in this thrilling magical adventure!

Find out more at: NicoleRTaylorWrites.com

See what titles are FREE at: Nicole's Free Reads

9 781922 624093